Uncle Terrible

"... he crouched down and brought his ear close to Uncle Terrible ..."

BOOK THREE

Uncle Terrible

More Adventures of Anatole

by Nancy Willard

ILLUSTRATIONS BY DAVID McPHAIL

Decorative letters by Sarah E. Knowles

HARCOURT BRACE JOVANOVICH, PUBLISHERS

SAN DIEGO   NEW YORK   LONDON

Requests for permission to make copies of any part of the work should be mailed to:
Permissions, Harcourt Brace Jovanovich, Publishers,
Orlando, Florida 32887

The verse on page 53 is reprinted and adapted by permission of Albyn Press, Edinburgh,
from their book *Hallowe'en* by F. Marian McNeill.
The verses on pages 37, 43, and 47 are reprinted and adapted by permission of Dover
Publications from their book *The Gift to Be Simple* by Edward D. Andrews.

Library of Congress Cataloging in Publication Data
Willard, Nancy.   Uncle Terrible.
SUMMARY: Anatole is faced with the formidable task of
retrieving the thread of death from the wizard Arcimboldo.
[1. Fantasy]   I. McPhail, David M., ill.   II. Title.
PZ7.W6553Un   1982   [Fic]   82-47940
ISBN 0-15-292793-X
ISBN 0-15-292794-8 (Voyager/HBJ : Pbk.)

Printed in the United States of America

BCDE
ABCDE(pbk.)

For Jerry, who loves Shakespeare and Spiderman

Uncle Terrible

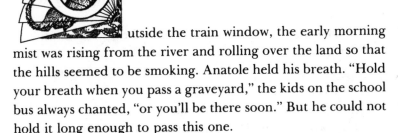utside the train window, the early morning mist was rising from the river and rolling over the land so that the hills seemed to be smoking. Anatole held his breath. "Hold your breath when you pass a graveyard," the kids on the school bus always chanted, "or you'll be there soon." But he could not hold it long enough to pass this one.

"Is that Himmel Hill?" asked a nun seated across the aisle, and she pointed out Anatole's window.

"Sure is," said the conductor. "We don't stop there if we can help it."

Then they rushed into total darkness. Anatole's mouth felt dry, and his father's words, as he waved good-by, came back to him: "If Uncle Terrible isn't there when the train pulls in, call your mother and me right away."

Anatole opened his knapsack, took out his comics, and

counted them. Six comics: *Thor, Spiderman, Captain America, The Legion of Superheroes, The Fantastic Four, The Incredible Hulk.* All in mint condition. Uncle Terrible would accept them, read them, and return them to Anatole. And maybe he would give Anatole some of the comics he bought for himself.

The train stopped so abruptly that everyone lurched forward. There was a general scramble for suitcases. Anatole clutched his knapsack and followed the nun into the aisle, where a throng of passengers was moving slowly toward the door.

"You have quite a collection of comics," she observed, smiling down at him.

"They're not mine," said Anatole. "They're a present for Uncle Terrible."

The nun stared at him. "How old is your uncle?"

"He's not my uncle. He's a family friend. And he's—grown up," added Anatole, realizing that he did not know Uncle Terrible's age.

"What did you say your friend's name was?" she asked.

"Uncle Terrible. Because—" and now it was Anatole's turn to smile—"because he's so terribly nice."

Anatole watched her step down to the platform and disappear into the crowd of strangers, and suddenly he felt he had lost his last friend. He touched his back pocket to check on his glasses. "Four eyes, four eyes," the kids at school called him. He had quit wearing them after that, but he always carried them.

"Is someone meeting you?" asked the conductor as he helped Anatole down the steps.

"Yes. No—I—"

Among the bustle of passengers getting off, somebody was hurrying down the platform toward the train and combing his thick black hair with his fingers: a large man, in faded jeans, a tweed jacket, a shirt as red as a fire truck, and rainbow suspenders, into which he had tucked his black beard like an ascot.

"Uncle Terrible!"

The man lurched forward, seized Anatole under the arms, and lifted him into a hug. His beard was as soft as a cat and smelled of cigars.

"Thank goodness you've come," said Uncle Terrible. "The apartment is like a tomb. An Egyptian tomb, crammed with treasures. This morning I actually lost myself between the kitchen and the bedroom. Anatole, where would you look for your Self if you lost it?"

He took Anatole's hand as they walked so that they would not be parted by the men and women rushing past them.

"I've invented a new game, Anatole. This is your Self—" and Uncle Terrible held up a gold button with a lion embossed on it. "Now, close your eyes. In which of my one hundred pockets have I hidden you?"

"Let's find a quieter place to play, Uncle Terrible," suggested Anatole.

"We'll play at lunch," said Uncle Terrible.

Outside the station, warm rain was beginning to fall. Everyone except Anatole and Uncle Terrible scurried for shelter. The two friends strolled past the shops, ducking from awning to awning. A few windows still showed masks and paper pumpkins, though Halloween had come and gone two weeks before.

They passed a window, empty of all but the sign:

MAMA'S HEROS, HOTDOGS, SUBMARINES

"Closed," said Uncle Terrible. "What a shame!"

In the window of the bar next door, Tarzan burst into light over the pinball machine. Bells clanged, balls clattered and spun, bim! bim! Through the half-open door drifted a strong smell of beer.

"For lunch," said Uncle Terrible, "I fancy a chocolate cat."

Anatole half expected Uncle Terrible to pull a chocolate cat from one of his pockets. But instead, his friend paused in front of a revolving door and pushed Anatole gently ahead of him.

After the bustle of the street, the boy was glad to sit at one of the small tables, close to a showcase of corn muffins and chocolate cats. The coffee shop was full of people. They sipped their coffee or waited in line at the counter, for this was a bakery as well as a coffee shop. Two girls behind the counter drew string from a golden ball that hung from the ceiling, with which they tied parcel after parcel, quick as shoelaces.

"Your order, sir," a plump girl said to Uncle Terrible.

Uncle Terrible ordered two chocolate cats and a bowl of whipped cream. As the girl started to leave, he called after her, "And bring me one of those apples from the bowl on the counter, please."

Then he turned to Anatole. "I mustn't neglect your health, or your mother won't let you visit me again. Now, where did I put that gold button?"

He took off his jacket. The lining drooped with pockets, and pockets lined the front of his vest, so that he seemed to be full of doors, like an apartment building.

"What a wonderful vest!" said Anatole, quite forgetting about the gold button.

"Do you like it?" asked Uncle Terrible, quite forgetting about it also. "It was knitted for me by a tailor on twelve golden needles. His grandfather got them from the emperor of China. Ah, the apple has arrived."

"Aren't you having an apple, Uncle Terrible?"

"I shall have a little nibble of yours."

He took a very small bite, as if he were eating poison.

Anatole shivered. "It's my wet sneakers," he thought, and he could almost hear his mother saying, "Anatole, didn't I tell you to wear your boots?" At that moment he felt a tap on his shoulder.

A man with red hair and a red beard and a long neck was bending toward him, holding out a paper fan of the sort that does not conveniently fold into one's pocket, and the way he

"... he ... reminded Anatole of a heron that ... cocks its head
and scans the water for fish."

hunched into his shabby fur coat reminded Anatole of a heron that crooks its neck and cocks its head and scans the water for fish.

One side of the fan was painted with dragons, the other with this brief message:

I AM A FAN OF ARCIMBOLDO THE MARVELOUS,
179 WEST BROADWAY.
YOUR WISH IS MY COMMAND.
MAGIC SHOWS EVERY NIGHT, 7 AND 9.

"You do not feel the need of a fan now," said the stranger, "but later, on a hot day, when all creation can scarcely draw a breath, you will remember your fan, and you will fan yourself, slowly at first, then faster and faster, and you will thank Arcimboldo from the bottom of your heart. I am Arcimboldo the Marvelous."

At the next table, an old woman was setting a shopping bag on the table. Her fur coat was all tight gray curls—just as if it had gotten a permanent, thought Anatole. She plunked herself into a chair, kicked off her boots, and massaged her bare feet.

"I came in all the way from Brooklyn to pick up my new dress, and it's still not ready," she said to Uncle Terrible, just as if they were old friends. "Cicero Yin is a good tailor, but is he worth it?" She turned to Arcimboldo. "Sometimes I wish I had wings instead of feet."

Arcimboldo the Marvelous muttered to himself. It sounded

to Anatole like "I want my dinner" or "I'm growing thinner."
To Anatole's astonishment, the woman vanished before his
eyes, like a flame that Arcimboldo had blown out. A little brown
and white barn owl hopped from her empty chair to the table
and cried in a mournful voice, "Whooooooooo! Whooooooooo!"

All around them, people shielded their faces with their arms,
and the girls wrapping parcels behind the counter sank to their
knees in terror.

"Open the door!"

The door was flung open, and the owl circled the room twice
and flew out into the world.

When Anatole glanced around for Arcimboldo the Marvelous, the old man, too, was gone.

he city is full of magic," said Uncle Terrible, "but rest assured, Anatole, that women do not turn into birds. Perhaps it flew in from the kitchen." He paused on the dark landing and puffed a little. "That was stair number eighty-eight. We have eleven more to go."

Anatole leaned over the banister. It wound down, down, like a far-off road, all the way back to the first floor. A milky light sifted through the skylight overhead, where someone had hung a dozen spider plants that trailed their branches toward them.

At the top of the last landing were two doors.

"Mine's the left one," said Uncle Terrible.

He took a large key from one of his pockets and fitted it into the lock.

"Why do you have two keyholes, one so high up?"

"You mean the peephole? That shows me who's on the other

side of the door before I open it," replied Uncle Terrible. "Open sesame!"

And with a turn of the key, the door sprang open.

"Behold," said Uncle Terrible.

In the middle of the room, rising out of a sea of newspapers, old grocery bags, and dirty laundry, stood a doll's house. It was taller than Anatole; it was nearly as tall as Uncle Terrible himself. Built of rosy brick, it had a widow's walk on the roof and a front door, dark blue, with a round brass knocker that glimmered like a friendly moon, and French doors tall enough to walk through—if you were small enough.

"Oh, Uncle Terrible!"

"A gift from an unknown admirer," said Uncle Terrible. "I found it on the fire escape. I asked around the building if anyone had lost a house, but no one claimed it. Welcome to my quiet retreat from—" And he waved his arms at the disorder of the apartment, as if he were commanding it to disappear.

"Let me show you around," he said, and he took a very small key from a very small pocket in his vest and unlocked the front door of the little house. The door did not open. But the entire front of the house swung open, like the door of a cupboard.

Anatole could scarcely believe his eyes. Three master bedrooms, each with a canopy bed, and a living room with a ruby glass chandelier and a sofa upholstered in red silk, and a large kitchen painted in red, white, and blue, and a bathroom

—why, the bathtub was *gold*! It crouched on four feet that ended in silver claws.

The most remarkable room was the library, just off the kitchen. At the table in the center, a dozen mice could have dined in comfort and afterward stretched out on the purple plush carpet for a nap, or curled up in one of the two armchairs, upholstered in leather. To Anatole's delight, the bookshelves were crammed with books, yet the largest volume was no bigger than a postage stamp. The boy took down a green one and opened it. The cover was soft and brilliant as moss, and the lines of the text lay close together, like strands of hair.

"Uncle Terrible, have you a magnifying glass?"

"I have no magnifying glass strong enough for that book. Put it back."

He sounded so disturbed that Anatole felt he should never have asked. For the first time that day, he wanted to go home. Uncle Terrible broke the silence between them.

"If you want to wash up for dinner—" He touched a faucet in the bathroom, and a pearly thread of water flowed into the silver sink. "Hot and cold," he announced proudly. "The stove in the kitchen works too. You can cook a small dinner for one large person, or a large dinner for six small persons. And in the evening—" He pressed a button in the living room, and the whole house lit up from top to bottom. The ruby chandelier glittered, throwing tiny rainbows on the ceiling like confetti.

"I used to have *two* chandeliers," Uncle Terrible observed. "The other was made of emerald glass. One night the emerald chandelier simply vanished. Make yourself at home, Anatole. I have to straighten up the outside world."

And he bustled about the big room, stuffing clothes into drawers, pushing boxes into closets, and as if by magic there came into view a four-foot inflatable King Kong by the front door and a Frankenstein mask on the wall and a comfortable jumble of overstuffed chairs and a floor lamp with an awful tasseled shade and an African violet on a pedestal and a red plush sofa that reminded Anatole of a kindly old man with a sagging belly.

Just in front of the little house, something gleamed through a knot in the floorboards. Anatole put his eye to it. To his disappointment, another eye did not meet his.

"Uncle Terrible, you have a blue marble under your floor. Let's rescue it."

Uncle Terrible shook his head. "We'd have to pry up the boards, and that would disturb the cockroaches. I sweep all my cookie crumbs into that crack, and the cockroaches never bother me. We've had the arrangement for years."

"May I call them cockroaches too, Uncle Terrible?"

"Why, what else would you call them?"

"Mom calls them Martian mosquitoes. If you say, 'I just saw a

Martian mosquito in the kitchen,' nobody will know you have cockroaches."

"But why shouldn't people know? Everybody in the city has cockroaches. The people who think they don't have them have the polite kind that mind their own business. Let me show you your bedroom. It connects to the bathroom. You won't mind my tiptoeing past you during the night? Give me your knapsack."

Beside the brass bed in the back room was a roll-top desk. Wham! Uncle Terrible, who was a high school Latin teacher, pulled the top down on a Latin dictionary and a clutter of papers, and now the room was perfectly tidy.

"A lovely view of the fire escape," said Uncle Terrible, pointing to the window. "And if you want a night light, you can borrow my Statue of Liberty."

There she stood, on top of the desk, gazing out the window.

"Can I pick her up?"

"Of course. Can you read the fine print on the base?"

Anatole read it easily: "*Give me your tired, your poor, your huddled masses yearning to breathe free.*"

"You know, the first penny I ever earned came from my Polish grandmother," said Uncle Terrible, "and she gave it to me for learning the rest of that poem by heart."

"Poem?" said Anatole, puzzled.

Uncle Terrible gravely recited it:

"Not like the brazen giant of Greek fame,
   With conquering limbs astride from land to land;
   Here at our sea-washed, sunset gates shall stand
   A mighty woman with a torch, whose flame
   Is the imprisoned lightning, and her name
   Mother of Exiles. From her beacon-hand
   Glows world-wide welcome; her mild eyes command
   The air-bridged harbor that twin cities frame.
   'Keep, ancient lands, your storied pomp!' cries she
   With silent lips. 'Give me your tired, your poor,
   Your huddled masses yearning to breathe free,
   The wretched refuse of your teeming shore.
   Send these, the homeless, tempest-tost to me.
   I lift my lamp beside the golden door!'"

"Very nice," said Anatole, though he was not sure he understood it.

"Now I want you to listen carefully, Anatole," said Uncle Terrible. "We're clean out of milk, and I'm going to the store at the end of the block. I won't be gone more than twenty minutes. Don't open the door to anyone but me."

"I promise," agreed Anatole. "Can I play with the little house?"

"Yes. But don't turn anything on. And don't touch the books. Here. Have a stick of bubble gum."

"My mom said—"

"It's sugarless," said Uncle Terrible.

"Thanks," said Anatole, and he popped the gum in his mouth.

As he knelt by the little house, he could hear Uncle Terrible humming his favorite tune, "Blue Moon." His footsteps grew fainter and fainter. Anatole opened the door of the oven and discovered a pile of dirty dishes. The plates were the size of buttons, the coffee pot no taller than a thimble. To Anatole's suprise, the oven was warm.

But he had promised he wouldn't turn on the oven, or the stove, or the lights, or the water.

But he could explore the apartment. Where would Uncle Terrible sleep? On the sofa, probably. He had given Anatole his own bed.

Anatole opened the door nearest the sofa. Uncle Terrible's jackets hung in a row, like a parade of ghosts. The smell of cigars still clung to them. How funny to have so many jackets! Anatole had only his windbreaker with the souvenir patches. None of Uncle Terrible's jackets had souvenir patches.

He opened a high thin door in the kitchen, and a little ironing board dropped out as far as its hinge would allow and struck him on the shoulder.

He opened the door beside the awful tasseled lamp, and a bed sprang out. It too was fixed at one end of the wall. So this was where Uncle Terrible slept. Anatole pushed the bed up, and to his relief it folded itself away obligingly, and he shut the door on it.

He opened a fourth door beside the pot-bellied sofa. Ah, this was where Uncle Terrible kept his comics! Four columns of comics that reached all the way to Anatole's waist. He sat down on the floor and plucked one from the top of the neatest column. *What if Doctor Strange had served Dormammu instead of the Ancient One?*

Mint condition. He turned to the first story.

Thump, thump.

What if Uncle Terrible came back and found him messing up his comics?

Thump.

But that wasn't a footstep on the stairs. The noise came from the opposite direction.

Thump.

From his room.

Thump, thump.

He shoved the comics into the closet, jumped up, and was just closing the door when a high voice outside the window sang,

> "My father is a butcher,
> My mother cuts the meat,
> And I'm a little wienie
> That runs around the street.
> How many times
> Did I run around the street?
> One, two, three—"

Anatole ran into his bedroom, unlocked the window, pushed it open, and crawled out on the fire escape. Drops of rain hung glistening from the railing. A tiger cat stared at him with sad eyes as if to warn him, *"Go back, go back, home is best,"* before it scampered away.

At the top of the fire escape, a girl in her nightgown was skipping rope. When she caught sight of Anatole, she called down, "I heard you talking. Are you sick, too?"

"No," Anatole called back.

"Why aren't you in school?"

"We're on holiday. What's wrong with you?"

"I have the flu!" shouted the girl. "And I'm so bored. When Grandma comes back from the store, I'll have to go back to bed."

Skip, skip.

"My name is Rosemarie, and my grandma has a garden on the roof. Come on up. I'm mostly well."

Anatole paused, halfway up the stairs.

"Uncle Terrible told me not to let any strangers in the house."

"Grandma told me the same thing," said the girl. "We'll play outside."

She darted back up to the roof, her black braids blowing behind her.

The fire escape shook so violently that Anatole did not dare look down, for he could see through the steps into the alley nine flights below.

"The roof," said the girl, "is the best place of all."

There were tubs of geraniums and pots of chives. Both grew as thick as in his mother's garden at home, and just such a pebbly path led through her garden as snaked among the pots and tubs in this one.

But his mother did not have a stone table and two wooden benches and half a great blue tub turned on its end with the Virgin Mary inside holding out her hands, and his mother didn't have a grape arbor, thickly woven with stems and bunches of grapes, both green and purple, hanging inside. Anatole reached for a grape, but the girl grabbed his arm.

"They're not real," she said. "But our doves are real. Come and see our doves."

The doves lived in a snug little tower like a pagoda. It had hundreds of windows through which the doves could come and go, though none were to be seen just then. But Anatole could hear them, cooing inside, and when the girl opened the door, there sat the doves on their nests, some white, some brown, and each family in its own room. The birds blinked at the children and clucked and scolded, and the girl closed the door again.

"I saw an owl in a coffee shop today," said Anatole. "And I met a magician. He gave me a fan with dragons on it."

He was tempted to add that he had seen a woman turn into that owl before his very eyes, but Uncle Terrible had said women never turned into birds. She *had* disappeared though. Very likely into the ladies' room.

"Anatole reached for a grape, but the girl grabbed his arm."

"An owl? Was it tame?"

"No, it flew outside."

"Maybe we'll see it," said the girl.

From the garden they could look out over other rooftops into a forest of television antennas and ventilation shafts. They could look right into other people's windows. They could look down at the cars, small enough to fit in their hands. Then they could look beyond the buildings to the river and the train tracks and the turrets of Himmel Hill.

Close by, bells began to chime. The girl pointed across the street to a church and a schoolyard next door. Children were running in from recess.

"That's my school," said the girl. "I hate it. We aren't allowed to talk during lunch, and we have to say catechism every morning with Sister Helen."

Suddenly Anatole caught sight of a familiar figure in a tweed jacket and a red shirt and rainbow suspenders crossing the street toward them.

"I have to go home," he said, "right now."

As he ran down the steps, the girl called after him, "I've always wanted a fan with dragons on it."

"I'll leave it for you on the fire escape," Anatole called over his shoulder.

After a frantic search, he spied the fan behind the little house. He stuck it to the fire escape with his bubble gum and was fumbling with the lock on the window when he heard someone fumbling with the lock on the door and Uncle Terrible strode into the apartment, his arms full of groceries. Anatole hurried to meet him.

"I've been thinking," exclaimed Uncle Terrible, "that it's a great afternoon to visit the Guinness Book of World Records Museum. And we can take dinner at a little place I know that serves the best spaghetti in town."

After dinner Anatole was tired but also content, for it isn't every day you can try on the belt of the fattest man and afterward eat all the spaghetti you want for supper. Though at home he never went to bed before nine, he did not object when at seven o'clock Uncle Terrible announced bedtime for both of them and unfolded his own bed in the living room. He graciously accepted Anatole's gift of comics and promised to let Anatole pick six from his own collection, in fair trade. He had left a book on mummies by Anatole's bed and a silver bell and a glass of milk and a box of Fig Newtons, and he told the boy he could turn on the Statue of Liberty and sleep in his clothes, including his baseball cap, and he could read as late as he liked.

But he must stay in his room. On no account should he open his door after eight o'clock.

In an emergency he might ring the bell.

Yes, that was fine with Anatole. He pulled on his jacket and climbed into bed, examined all the photographs of mummies in the book, thought how much he would like to have one, and turned off the overhead light. He thought how delightful Latin would be if he had Uncle Terrible for a teacher. The Statue of Liberty glowed, as if a star had fallen into the room.

If he were home, his father would sing to him before he turned off the light.

"Get on board, little children," Anatole sang to himself, since there was no one to sing it for him.

He dozed off at last.

He had scarcely fallen asleep when a clap of thunder woke him—bang! bang! The rain roared down, the window blew open, the door flew open, and Anatole jumped out of bed to close it.

What was that faint light in the living room? Was Uncle Terrible awake? Was he ill? No, not ill.

He crept into the living room. The light came from the little house.

CHAPTER THREE

I n the little house, Uncle Terrible sat at the kitchen table humming "Blue Moon" and holding the moss-green book in his hand. He was shading it with a bouquet.

"Why, that's the book he told me nobody could read," said Anatole. And he rushed forward. "Uncle Terrible, make me small too!"

The tiny gentleman sprang from his chair.

"Make me small, too, Uncle Terrible. Make me small, too!"

Uncle Terrible's legs seemed to fold under him. He sank into his chair, clutching his head. Presently he turned to Anatole and spoke, but alas!—his voice was as small as his person. Anatole could scarcely hear him, though he crouched down and brought his ear close to Uncle Terrible, who raised himself on tiptoes and rested one hand on Anatole's ear lobe to steady himself.

"If you promise me that you will never, never tell anyone, I shall reveal my secret," said the faint, whiskery voice of Uncle Terrible.

"I promise," said Anatole.

"Please don't shout."

"I'm not shouting," said Anatole. "This is my normal voice."

"It is not normal to me," squeaked Uncle Terrible. "Now listen closely—and stay away from that crack in the floor. On the first page of this book you will find some lines written in an unknown tongue. Read them out loud."

"But you said I couldn't—"

"I said you couldn't read them with a magnifying glass. You can read them by the light of these flowers."

Anatole took the flowers from Uncle Terrible. Cornflowers and clover, they gave off a faint fragrance that reminded him of a place he had known long ago but could not quite recall. He opened the book, held the flowers over the first page, and found that he could read the text perfectly.

> "Woneka, wonodo,
> Eka mathaka rata," said Anatole.

There rose to his nostrils a delicious promise of toast.

> "A gbae se—"

He noticed that Uncle Terrible was covering his ears, and he lowered his voice.

> "Dombra, dombra, dombra."

Fall, small, and away! Anatole gazed around in astonishment at the cupboard, the table, the stove, and the grill, on which half a dozen sandwiches were sizzling. Uncle Terrible was tucking the bouquet into the pages of the book.

"Would you like a toasted cheese?" he asked. "I'm simply famished."

If the little house seemed wonderful before, it was ten times more wonderful now when Anatole turned and looked back at the apartment. The awful tasseled lamp shaded the little house like an ancient tree; the hooked rug unfolded range upon range of hills and valleys like waves lapping away into the darkness.

"Uncle Terrible," said Anatole, "are you a magician?"

"No," said Uncle Terrible. "I'm just lucky."

He arranged the sandwiches on a plate and carried them to the kitchen table and drew up stools for Anatole and himself.

"The day after my other chandelier disappeared, some unknown benefactor left this book on my shelf. When I opened it, the bouquet of pressed flowers fell out, and when I picked up the flowers, they came alive in my hand, and I discovered the book was magic."

Uncle Terrible took a large bite of his sandwich.

"What other spells can the book do?" asked Anatole, who was much too excited to eat.

"That's what I'd like to know," said Uncle Terrible, chewing. "Every night I read it to myself—I don't dare read it aloud any more—but I can't crack the code. It's not Latin, it's not Greek, it's not Finnish or Sanskrit. Come—let me show you something you'll like."

And he ushered Anatole into the library. A checkerboard was set up on the center table.

"I love checkers," said Anatole.

They drew up chairs, and Anatole had just made the opening move when they both heard a rustling in the kitchen. Uncle Terrible stood up, and Anatole stood up, and they tiptoed to the door.

Nobody there. But the thud of something being lugged over the floor could be heard in the living room. Anatole felt as if his heart were pounding in his throat. Nevertheless, he followed Uncle Terrible into the living room.

A cockroach in a turban of wrapped tinsel, a tinsel skirt, and a gray cloak was trying to fasten a broken candle to the hook that had once held the missing chandelier. She had made a loop in the wick to hang it by, but one claw held something under her cloak as she worked, and this greatly hampered her. The other she snapped and clicked: the sound sent shivers up Anatole's spine.

"Bring back my chandelier!" shouted Uncle Terrible.

With a volley of loud squeaks, the cockroach leaped out of the house and fled into the darkness of the apartment. Anatole was certain he had never seen any creature as monstrous as this one.

"What a mess!" said Uncle Terrible. "Crumbs all over. I suppose she helped herself in the kitchen."

The grilled cheese sandwiches were gone.

"I'd feel safer if I were my own size again," said Anatole.

"I understand perfectly," said Uncle Terrible. "Now, where did I put the magic book?"

Suddenly he glanced down and gave a shriek. "There it is—down the crack in the floor!"

Anatole knelt beside Uncle Terrible at the edge of the crack, which yawned vast as a canyon to them now.

"I don't see it," said Anatole.

"It was there a minute ago," said Uncle Terrible.

A thin slice of light gleamed up at them from under the floorboards.

"Let's tie the bed sheets into a rope," said Uncle Terrible, "and I shall lower you into the crack."

"Me!" exclaimed Anatole.

"My dear boy, there's nothing to fear. At the first tug, I shall draw you up."

It did not take them long to pull the sheets off the beds and knot them together. Anatole grasped one end, and Uncle Terrible held the other and lowered him down, down through the crack, till the boy's feet rested on a pile of dust, not far from the blue marble.

Oh, how big the little space in the crack looked to him now! Beyond the blue marble lay a low counter, and behind the

"Beyond the blue marble lay a low counter, and behind the counter dozed the cockroach . . ."

counter dozed the cockroach, still wearing her turban of wrapped tinsel and her gray fur coat, which had once belonged to a mouse. Sandwich crumbs clung to her feelers, which drooped across her front legs; she had fallen asleep reading a moss-green book that Anatole recognized only too well. He found himself more curious than frightened.

A silver ring in the shape of a snake sparkled on a shelf directly over her head.

"That ring is much too large for a cockroach," said Anatole, forgetting that in his present shape it was also much too large for him.

He reached over the sleeping cockroach and took down the ring. Neatly inked on a stamp hinge attached to the ring were the words:

FINDERS KEEPERS

"I've found it, so I'll keep it," said Anatole. He slipped the serpent ring over his arm. "If Uncle Terrible says I ought not to keep it, I can always send it down the crack."

Over the cockroach's head glowed an emerald chandelier, the very match of that hanging in the living room of the little house, and its light showed Anatole shelf upon shelf—he couldn't see the end of them, for they seemed to stretch into infinity—and they were crammed with paper clips, postage stamps, holy medals, razor blades tied in packets of a dozen or so, two plastic grapes that Anatole recognized as having come from the roof garden, and assorted marbles, mostly cat's-eyes and aggies, smaller than the blue marble, though just as beautiful.

From the top shelf hung a sign:

THE TRADING POST
OPEN ALL NIGHT

And below it, embroidered in purple thread on a scrap of lavender silk:

THOU SHALT NOT STEAL

Anatole picked up a smoky-glass marble. Tiny gold stars glittered deep at the heart, like lights at the bottom of a well. The price tag read:

2 CENTS

"I'll send two pennies down the crack tomorrow," said Anatole, and he took the marble.

Then he laid hands on the book.

"It can't be stealing, since the book belongs to Uncle Terrible."

Holding his breath, he slid the book very slowly out from under the head and bristly legs of the sleeping cockroach. Then he hurried back to the blue marble and grabbed the bed sheet.

"Uncle Terrible, Uncle Terrible—pull me up!"

Greatly excited, Uncle Terrible jerked the rope so hard that

Anatole dropped the glass marble, which clattered against the blue one, and both rolled past the counter toward the far end of the shop.

The cockroach lifted her head in time to see the boy's feet disappear over the edge of the crack. "Thief! Thief!" she cried.

A general scratching and scuttling answered her in the upper world of the apartment. From the darkness under beds and the darkness under bureaus, from the darkness under the icebox and the darkness under the stove marched the cockroaches, hundreds upon hundreds, and each cockroach carried an open safety pin, and the pins glittered, and the popping eyes of the cockroaches glittered, and they surged into the living room like a wave wearing diamonds on its back.

"Uncle Terrible, hurry! Say the spell!"

Uncle Terrible seized the book and clutched the bouquet over it.

> *"Woneka, wonodo,*
> *Eka mathaka rata,*
> *A gbae se*
> *Dombra, dombra, dombra."*

As Uncle Terrible soared to his full height, he tossed both book and bouquet to Anatole, who caught them and read,

> *"Woneka, wonodo."*

At which one cockroach, larger than the rest, shouted, "Brothers and sisters, attack!"

Fifty cockroaches leaped on the boy and tried to grab the book. Anatole hung on, and while the cockroaches pulled and tugged, he managed to keep both book and bouquet out of their reach and to shout,

"*Eka mathaka rata*
A gbae se
Dombra, dombra, dombra,"

just as the page tore and the biggest cockroach fled through the crack with the book between his teeth and the flowers between his feelers, and all the cockroaches poured after him like sand sifting down a hole.

And now, silence. Still trembling, Anatole switched on the tasseled lamp in the living room of the apartment. Uncle Terrible was sitting on the sofa, his eyes closed, his palm on his forehead.

"I lost the book, Uncle Terrible," said Anatole, "but I saved this ring."

He handed the ring to Uncle Terrible. What a cunning silver serpent it was, bright and modest as starlight.

Uncle Terrible tipped it this way and that, till the light caught an inscription on the inside:

IF LOST, TURN TO THE WRIGHT
WRIGHT'S SUPERIOR TOFFEES LTD.

"A souvenir of Anatole's battle with the Martian mosquitoes," said Uncle Terrible as he slipped the ring over his own right pinky. "There now, we won't lose it. What we need, Anatole, is some hot chocolate to revive us after our ordeal."

The ring glimmered and shimmered and wreathed his finger so exactly like a real snake that Anatole couldn't resist stroking it, for he was fond of snakes and often kept garter snakes as pets. He stroked it once. Twice.

On the third stroke, an extraordinary change came over Uncle Terrible. His body pulled itself out like taffy and gathered itself to the thickness of Anatole's wrist. The rainbow suspenders and the red shirt dissolved to an iridescent shimmer on the gorgeous skin of a snake that lifted its head and met Anatole's astonished gaze. The ring clattered to the floor. Uncle Terrible no longer had hands to hold it.

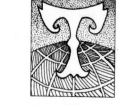he snake made a sound like steam hissing and darted its tongue in an experimental sort of way.

"Oh, Uncle Terrible," cried Anatole, "I'm sorry!"

"Sssssorry, ssssorrrry," breathed the snake and draped itself around the boy's shoulder. It had Uncle Terrible's face, right down to his black beard, only the face was small as an apple and peered out from a hood of glittering scales.

"Sssssave the ssssssilver ssssssserpent," hissed Uncle Terrible.

"I don't know how to save you," wailed Anatole.

"The ssssssilver ssssssserpent," repeated Uncle Terrible.

"The ring?"

Anatole picked it up and read the inscription aloud once more. " 'If lost, turn to the Wright.' I'm not lost, Uncle Terrible, but you are. So I'll turn to—to the right."

He turned and found himself facing the mirror.

"Maybe I should turn the ring to the right?"

And he slipped the ring over his finger.

"Sssssstop," warned Uncle Terrible, but Anatole was already twisting it.

The light in the little house gathered itself into a beam that shone straight into the mirror, like a road. And there in the mirror itself—what was that prick of light advancing slowly, like a train at the far end of a tunnel? He squinted, shaded his eyes, and gave a gasp of delight.

A stagecoach, no higher than his knee, was jogging toward him. It was made of moss and drawn by a ghostly mule. Smoke wrapped around a ladder of bones; you could see right through him.

"Why, there's no driver," exclaimed Anatole, for he saw none.

But who else could be singing so loud and joyously?

"Great eye, little eye, great eye can see,
    Little eye is sharp eye, little I will be.
    Little eye, simple eye, little eye is free,
    Little eye is sharp eye, little I will be."

Swaying to and fro on the driver's seat, a star-nosed mole was beating time with the reins, though he was scarcely as big as the boy's hand, which is bigger than most moles but smaller than most drivers. On the side of the coach facing Anatole, forget-me-nots grew in the shape of a sign:

MOTHER'S TAXI

BY APPOINTMENT TO DAME KIND

NO SPELL TOO LARGE   NO FOLK TOO SMALL

"All aboard," called the mole. "Plenty of room inside."

He dropped the reins, and the mule halted above the pedestal, just over Uncle Terrible's African violet. The coach rested so easily on the air that it might have stood on a well-traveled road. The mule stretched forth his neck to browse among the blossoms and pawed the air as if he felt under him the lush grass of an invisible pasture.

"I didn't call a taxi," said Anatole.

The mole peered at Anatole over his pince-nez, from which a black ribbon dangled, thin as a whisker.

"Didn't an enchantment take place?" asked the mole.

"It sure did," said Anatole. "Uncle Terrible accidentally turned himself into a snake. But I didn't call a taxi."

"Whenever an enchantment takes place," said the mole, "it rings up the main office, and I'm sent out. I'm the porter, taxi driver, stretcher-bearer, and comforter, all in one. Are *you* enchanted, lad?"

Anatole shook his head.

"Then you can ride up on the driver's box with me."

The mole scampered down and opened the door of the coach; the moist fragrance of a summer night breathed out of it.

"Sssssssssir," began Uncle Terrible, but the mole interrupted him.

"Can't talk, eh? Once we get moving, you'll find your voice. In you go, my scaly friend."

Uncle Terrible flashed inside, and the door closed so seamlessly after him that you could not have told where to open it again. Anatole climbed up beside the mole, and found to his surprise that he was exactly the right size for the coach. The mole jerked the reins, and the mule lifted his head and trotted around the room at a brisk pace, still chewing. Yet the violets, Anatole noticed, were untouched.

"Aren't you going back through the mirror?" asked Anatole.

"Never go out the way you came in. It's in the rules."

"Whose rules?" asked Anatole.

"Mother's rules."

"Your mother made that rule?"

"She's not just *my* mother," said the mole.

"Whose mother is she?"

"When you meet her," said the mole, "you can see whose mother she is. Draw the curtain from the window behind you, lad."

Anatole did so and could not help smiling. In the coach Uncle Terrible lay curled up on an upholstery of fresh roses. On the opposite seat perched a brown and white owl.

"That passenger met Arcimboldo in a coffee shop on Tenth Street," said the mole. "She'd stopped at the tailor's to pick up a dress, and she was on her way back to Brooklyn. She told me that nobody's heard of Arcimboldo the Marvelous in Brooklyn, so of course she wasn't on her guard when they met."

Anatole remembered the woman with the tired feet in the coffee shop and said to himself, "So she really did turn into an owl."

"Now, the passenger sitting next to her had fair warning," continued the mole.

"There's nobody next to the owl," said Anatole.

"You are mistaken. The other passenger is invisible except for that little rope she carries. The poor girl was given a fan"—and here Anatole nearly fell off the box—"and it has Arcimboldo's name right on it, but do you think she took the slightest notice of that? No, indeed. She started fanning herself, and both she and the fan faded into thin air. He's not called Arcimboldo the Marvelous for nothing."

"Rosemarie!" exclaimed Anatole.

The coach sailed through the open window, over the fire escape.

"There, on the bottom step of the fire escape—that's where I left the fan for Rosemarie," thought Anatole.

The coach climbed steadily into the wind, and Anatole drew his jacket around him. Below him the roof garden lay dark and still, but the rest of the city, a patchwork of rectangles, was stitched with light.

"And how did your companion fall into an enchantment?" inquired the mole.

"Uncle Terrible? This ring did it," answered Anatole, and he held out his hand.

The mole glanced at the ring and said, "It's the same story everywhere. Arcimboldo loves to put spells on ordinary things. The toys in Crackerjack, the keys in people's pockets, the catsup in diners. He loves to make trouble. He loves to put innocent people under his spells. Once they're in his power, nobody ever sees them again."

The mole sighed, then turned shyly to Anatole. "Tell me, lad, do you know any stories? I dearly love stories."

"What kind of stories?" asked Anatole.

"True stories," said the mole.

"Let me tell you what happened to me and Uncle Terrible tonight," said Anatole, and he told the mole all about the little house and the magic book, and how a cockroach in a turban snatched it, and how Anatole went after the book and lost it.

"I like the part about the book best," said the mole. "It's so mysterious, the way it appears in the library after Uncle Terrible loses his emerald chandelier."

"I suppose the cockroaches traded the one for the other," said Anatole. "The book must be one of Arcimboldo's tricks."

"Moss green, with flowers to light the pages? That's not Arcimboldo's book. This land was full of magic long before you and I came to live on it, and once in a blue moon something magic turns up. I suspect one of Mother's winds brought your companion his little house. Long ago on Himmel Hill, wonderful toys marked the graves of children, and living children played there, so the dead wouldn't be forgotten . . ." His voice dwindled away. He cleared his throat. "Don't miss the view."

They passed over the twin towers of the World Trade Center, as humble as salt and pepper shakers. Then the coach turned sharply and headed north.

"Where's the George Washington Bridge?" asked Anatole.

"Just where it always was," answered the mole. "But in Mother's taxi, we see by different lights. I follow the stars. Bridges come and bridges go, but the stars have been showing the way to Mother's house for thousands of years. You have a bird's-eye view, lad, and the birds see a great deal more than those who live on the ground."

Anatole peered down into the darkness. The land was all forest and pasture, and it seethed and rustled with life. Hundreds of creatures flowed across it; mice and ferrets, chipmunks and snakes. In the clearings, tortoises, coyotes, badgers, and woodchucks ran together. Deer leaped in herds, cougars loped side by side, and mountain goats ran peacefully alongside them.

Level with the coach, a flock of geese were winging north.

"Old honkers, aren't you flying the wrong way?" called the mole.

"Mother called us, Mother called us," answered the geese.

"Where are they going?" asked Anatole.

The coach sank slowly toward a hill crowned with white stones, some straight like steeples, some round and thin as slices of bread, and all standing silent like pieces in a game abandoned by giants.

"I hope we're not going to the graveyard," whispered Anatole.

The mole sang on over the squeaking and mewing and roaring and rumbling of the animals:

> "The least of Mother's errands
> is good enough for me.
> It's more than I am worthy of—"

as the coach floated over the iron gates and the mule's hooves brushed the tops of the gravestones.

> "I want nothing better.
> I'll not exchange it
> For anything greater."

Now they were skimming row upon row of American flags that marked the graves of the veterans of many wars. How skillfully the mole guided the mule between granite angels and moss-shrouded soldiers in heroic poses, and how gently the mule alighted before a plain marker of modest size, on which was inscribed in raised letters:

"... as the coach floated over the iron gates and the mule's hooves
brushed the tops of the gravestones."

MOTHER

The mule lifted his hoof and knocked three times on the stone. The animals crowded around him, the door of the coach swung open, and the scaly form of Uncle Terrible writhed out, followed by the owl.

"My dear Anatole," he whispered, "I've had a most interesting conversation with a young lady who claims that you made her invisible."

"I can speak for myself," said Rosemarie's voice close by.

"Hush," rumbled an elk. "Mother's coming."

The earth around the gravestones grew lighter and lighter, as if a fire burned in the heart of each of them.

"Windows!" exclaimed Anatole. "The ground is full of windows."

The windows, which kept the odd shapes of the stones themselves, looked right down into Mother's house. The shape of an angel gave Anatole a clear view of the living room. In the fireplace, so tall and deep that Anatole could have walked right into it, a lively flame was leaping and sending its smoke up through the ground.

And now the boy observed that the smoke of many fireplaces in many rooms was rising all over the graveyard, and he remembered noticing this smoke from the train window and mistaking it for mist.

The lamp on the great round table was carved from a

rutabaga, and the oil in the lamp threw such an amber light on the floor that the rushes scattered there seemed washed in honey.

"Do I spy a newspaper on the table?" asked Uncle Terrible. "Do I see *The Christian Science Monitor?* Who on earth brings you *The Christian Science Monitor?*"

"Nobody," said the mule. "It blew here years and years ago. Out of date, of course, but what does that matter? The creatures come. They can't read a newspaper, but they expect one, they want one. Especially the mice. They've worked in the lobbies of the best hotels, and they have their own notions of grandeur. Mother doesn't want to disappoint them."

"The bedrooms are even better than the living room," a bear murmured into Anatole's ear. "Mother has the best beds in the world, especially if you're planning to hibernate. She made them herself from the wood of the Himmel tree, and they tell the most lovely stories."

"Where do the Himmel trees grow?" asked Rosemarie's voice.

The bear gazed respectfully at the empty space that was Rosemarie.

"There are no more Himmel trees. The early settlers cut them down for cradles."

"And what language do the beds speak?" asked Uncle Terrible.

"Your language," replied the bear.

And Uncle Terrible, who did not hear well, said, "Ur language! I fear the stories would be lost on me."

Suddenly voices from within the house sang,

"Sweep the floor, sweep the floor,
Mother's hurrying toward the door."

A restlessness rippled through the creatures. The light from the stone bearing her name brightened into a door.

"Here comes Mother!" squeaked a raccoon.

All turned. A giant of a woman was striding toward them. The face that smiled out of her sunbonnet was as lumpy and plain as a potato. She wore corn shucks gathered into a gown, over which shimmered an apron of onion skins. Through her bonnet poked antlers that branched out like a tree, and at the end of every branch danced a flame, which lit the ground before her. She was carrying a wicker basket from which every now and then she threw a handful of white roses. The roses melted as soon as they touched the ground, and a thin glaze of frost sparkled in their place.

"Is my table set?" shouted Mother.

"Yes, Mother!" chorused hundreds of voices from within.

"Is my soup ready?"

"Yes, Mother!" called the voices as before.

"Then I'm ready," she answered, and through the door she crawled on all fours, with the animals and Anatole and Uncle Terrible and Rosemarie and the owl tumbling in after her.

round the stone table gathered the crea-tures, and when Mother took her place, a flurry of chipmunks actually scampered across the table and crowded into the folds of her gown.

"Would you prefer a seat among the snakes?" the mole asked politely.

"Certainly not," said Uncle Terrible.

An elk marched round and round, keeping order, especially among the rabbits, who were inclined to be rowdy. Anatole and Uncle Terrible and Rosemarie, whose skip rope was visible in her invisible hand, sat between the mole and the raccoon, both of whom kept a sharp eye on her place so that nobody would sit on her.

"Children, children, are you hungry?" said Mother.

A hubbub of squeaks and roars answered her, and the otters thumped their tails on the table. Mother walked around the table, and as she walked, she raised her right hand and out dropped suet for the cardinals, sunflower seeds for the chickadees, and thistle seeds for the finches. She raised it again, and a dozen bundles of hay dropped in front of the deer. She raised it again, and a mess of fish fell in front of the otters—oh, nobody was forgotten, nobody, nobody—and Mother bustled back and forth, encouraging the coyotes to take seconds and the eagle to clean his plate and the quails and the pheasants to try a new dish she had invented just for them.

When she came to Anatole, she stopped walking and clapped her hands for silence. "My dear children," said Mother, "we have among us three guests whom Arcimboldo the Marvelous has enchanted. I need not tell them what I must tell you, that we are all in grave danger."

A deep hush fell over the company.

"Since the beginning of time, I have worn at my waist two threads twisted into one, the thread of life and the thread of death. Every morning you have heard me sing the 'Song of Strong Knots' to keep them in place."

"Thank you, Mother," said the elk.

"Alas for us! One of my children gave Arcimboldo that song. And Arcimboldo learned it so well that he could sing it forward and backward. And when he sang it backward, the threads of life and death untwined themselves and flew into his hands."

"It was the cockroaches," the mole whispered to Anatole. "They generally sit near me, and they're absent."

"Now Arcimboldo has taken the thread of life to be knitted into a cloak," continued Mother. "When he puts on that cloak, I will be helpless to break his spells."

"Is there no one who can help us?" bellowed the old otter with gray whiskers.

Silence. Then a tiny voice piped up, "We spiders know, if we haven't forgotten."

A brown spider crawled to the middle of the table, and all the creatures leaned forward to listen.

"Our old lore says, Let a great hero win the thread of death, let the thread be knitted into a cloak, and let the cloak of death be joined to the cloak of life, and all whom Arcimboldo has enchanted will be whole again."

"Can you spiders do this?" asked Mother.

"Our old lore says, Whoever wants it must win it," squeaked the spider. "And the hero must be human."

Everybody looked at Anatole.

"You're human," said the otter. "You can't deny it."

"I'm no hero," said Anatole. "I'm scared stiff."

"Nobody is a hero before the quest," said Mother.

"And where will he find the cloak of life?" asked the mole.

"It is being knitted on the twelve golden needles of an innocent tailor who has no idea what a wonderful thread he's got under his roof," said Mother.

"Golden needles? It's not the tailor who lives on Tenth Street?" exclaimed Uncle Terrible.

"The very fellow," replied Mother.

"And maybe the only honest man in the city," said the spider. "Nobody who steals or lies can command the twelve golden needles."

"I know the fellow," said Uncle Terrible. "Anatole, take me with you."

"And take me, too," said Rosemarie. "I'm a great knitter. I can do cable stitch. And take the owl, she's very clever—why, where *is* the owl?"

But the owl who had chatted so amiably in the coach was nowhere to be found.

"Our old lore says that the great hero must go alone," said the spider.

"Oh, bother your old lore," hissed Uncle Terrible.

"Look here," said Anatole. "I don't even know where the magician lives."

Mother pointed to the fire.

"My fireplace is so deep that you can easily walk behind the flames. Anatole, tell me what you see behind the fire."

"A door," replied Anatole.

"Through that door," said Mother, "you will find a road. It will take you to my elder trees. And on my elder trees I hang my masks. From sunrise till dawn of the following day, you can be a jackal, a mouse, a wolf, a dove, a cat—whatever pleases you. Take only one. You will know the right time to wear it."

She folded her big hand around his small one and led him

"She folded her big hand around his small one and led him behind the flames . . ."

behind the flames, and he thought he had never been so hot in all his life. And there crouched the tiger cat he had seen on the fire escape outside Uncle Terrible's apartment.

"I didn't know *you*'d be here," said Anatole.

"Home is best," purred the cat.

When Mother pushed the door open, the smell of moss and clover cooled him a little.

"The road runs through my orchard and leads straight to the magician's house. My mule will take you to the border. You'll find him grazing in the orchard.

Anatole turned to say good-by, but Mother stopped him.

"Don't look back," she warned him.

The last sound he heard as he stepped through the door was the tiger cat wailing in a singsong voice,

> "Anatole will come, will come,
> Witchcraft will be set a-going;
> Wizards will be at full speed,
> Running in every pass.
> Avoid the road, children, children!"

The door hushed closed behind him. East, west, north—as far as he could see—grew apple trees. Their branches were laden with fruit, and under one of them, browsing in the tall grass for windfall apples, waited the ghost-mule.

"Walk or ride?" he inquired.

"I can walk, thank you," said Anatole, for the mule looked very tired.

"If I were in your shoes"—here the mule glanced down at Anatole's sneakers with their broken and knotted laces—"I'd ride. We've a long journey ahead of us. But suit yourself."

"If it's very long, I think I *will* ride," said Anatole, and the mule stooped and Anatole clambered on. The mule's back felt sharp as a saddle of sticks, and the boy thought he had never sat so uncomfortably in all his life.

"Take a little refreshment," said the mule, "where my heart used to be."

Anatole peered down into the mule's rib cage, and there, where his heart used to be, hung a little basket. He drew up the basket and found a sandwich, neatly wrapped in grape leaves, and a mug of hot soup.

"Mother put 'em there," said the mule. "I hope you like peanut butter?"

"Oh, very much," said Anatole.

"And the soup was made fresh today. She gives it only to travelers. It warms, it strengthens, and it doesn't spill."

Orioles and goldfinches glittered in the trees, meadowlarks and catbirds sang in the thickets, the tall grass trembled, and the daisies and cornflowers nodded as the travelers passed.

"I'm no end of convenience to Mother," the mule said, in pleased tones.

Anatole wiped his mouth on the back of his hand and was seized with remorse. "I'm so sorry—I forgot to offer you any," he said.

"No matter," said the mule. "I don't eat things, I just whiff off the fragrance, though when I had my flesh, I had appetite enough. My old master sold fish, and I pulled the wagon through good times and bad times. But it was always my wish to find Mother. And the last day of my life—awfully cold, it was—I opened my eyes and there was this giant of a woman lifting the gate to my stall. 'What do you want?' I says to her. 'A ride home,' she says to me. 'I can't carry you,' I says. 'Didn't say you had to,' she says, and she picks me up and tucks me under her arm and walks right out into the yard. I felt as light as a leaf, and she never put me down till we got home. And I've been a great convenience to her ever since."

Now the apple trees grew scarcer; they were entering a grove of elders. A wind shook the branches, and Anatole saw that what he had taken for leaves were masks: coyotes, badgers, tigers, elephants, toucans, pelicans, with empty spaces left for the eyes.

"Let's see what's left," mused the mule.

"Don't people steal them?" asked Anatole.

"Nobody comes here without Mother's leave," said the mule, "and once the masks are used, they always come home to Mother. What pleases you?"

The mule strolled under the trees so that Anatole could choose.

"I like the tiger," said Anatole.

"If I were in your skin," said the mule, "I'd pick the cat. Fierce but friendly. Small but quick. At home everywhere."

Anatole saw the wisdom of this and pulled off the mask of a black-and-white cat, which instantly shriveled itself into a thin loop around his wrist.

"When you need it, it'll be waiting for you. Mother's masks take care of themselves."

He trotted out of the grove into a sparse woods. And it seemed to Anatole that the trees were less friendly on this side, the air chillier. The sky shone red, as if the sun were setting.

"Red sky in the morning, sailors take warning," said Anatole.

"The sky is always red over Arcimboldo's house," observed the mule.

They were once again passing through an orchard. But no birds sang here, and no fragrance of flowers, or of apples crushed underfoot, delighted them. In the trees, made of steel with copper leaves, hung dozens of ruby balls. There was a smell of pennies hoarded in jars, the silence of jewels under glass.

"No matter how he tries," said the mule, "Arcimboldo can't make an orchard like Mother's. I can't go farther than this. His house is just beyond these trees."

Terror seized Anatole when he saw the mule was leaving him. "What will I say to Arcimboldo? What *can* I say? And how will I find the thread of death?"

"Our old lore says—" whispered a voice.

And the brown spider sprang to the top of the mule's head.

"Little brother!" exclaimed the mule, very much surprised. "Does Mother know you're here?"

"What does your old lore say?" asked Anatole.

"Our old lore says that the magician will ask you to play a game of checkers. Do you play checkers?"

"A little," faltered Anatole.

"Then you must outwit him. Arcimboldo's glasses let him peer around the corners of time. He can see your next move before you make it, and your next move, and your next. If you can get him to take off his glasses, you have a fair chance of winning. And if you win, ask for the thread of death."

"And what happens if I lose?"

"Don't ask," said the spider.

"But I want to know," said Anatole.

The spider brushed a sparkle of web off one leg.

> "This I learned from Mother's well.
> Fifteen years a mourning bell,"

buzzed the spider. "A bell in Arcimboldo's house. That's what you'll be."

A clatter of wings in a tree behind them made them turn in time to see the owl darting through the still branches.

"As the owl flies," said the spider, "you'll find the magician's house."

"The blessings of the sun and moon and rain and stars and snow and spiders and my old bones be upon you," said the mule. "And that's more than Arcimboldo has. Good-by."

hen he stepped into the clearing, Anatole found himself facing the oddest house he had ever seen. The outer wall was copper, engraved with hundreds of doors, and each door glowed as if burnished with secret fires. And what did the wall enclose? An enormous steel dome, without windows or chimneys or any sign of life.

As he walked around the wall, he couldn't help admiring the doors engraved on it, some plain, some overgrown with fruit and flowers drawn in the most meticulous detail. On one especially ornate door was incised a bellpull and a door knocker in the shape of a wreath.

"So many doors, and not one of them opens," Anatole said with a sigh.

No sooner had he spoken than the head of Arcimboldo grinned at him through the leaves of the wreath. "Ring the bell, Anatole, ring the bell," cackled the head.

Anatole felt a pair of claws grip his right shoulder. He spun round, terrified. Perched on his shoulder was the owl.

The boy now saw a real bell hanging on a copper ribbon. Before he could reach for it, the bell started to ring by itself, and as if waiting for that signal, bells began to ring around him, though he could see nary a one of them: families of church bells, choruses of dinner bells, sleigh bells, school bells, cowbells, ship bells, and bells that boomed out the hours in a hundred town clocks, all of them telling a different time, all of them invisible. And it seemed to Anatole that under the jangling he heard weeping. Over the ringing of the bells and the weeping roared the voice of Arcimboldo.

"Ring the bell, Anatole, ring the bell!"

This time Anatole gave the bell at the door a good hard tug. Instantly the ringing stopped. The head of Arcimboldo vanished. The engraved door opened, and Anatole felt himself pushed inside.

The room was very hot, and smooth and windowless as an egg. By the light of the seven giant rubies that hung from seven copper chains, the walls gleamed a fiery rose. There was not much furniture. In the middle of the room glimmered a little silver table and two benches, one encrusted with emeralds, the other with pearls. The checkerboard was also cut from emeralds and pearls, as well as the playing pieces. Against the far wall stood a copper chest, and next to that a fireplace, but no fire burned there.

"The bells, Anatole," said the owl on his shoulder.

Around the room, in midair, hung the bells—hundreds and hundreds. And in them he saw not his own reflection but the shapes of creatures that seemed to be hidden in the bells themselves. Bloodhounds and tomcats, rabbits and hedgehogs, a girl carrying a trombone, a man taking off his overcoat, a baby asleep in its stroller, robins and deer—rows and rows of them, silent in the fiery light.

Anatole sat down on the bench covered with pearls and longed for the strength of Superman, the web-slinging fingers of Spiderman, and the nimble feet of the Human Fly. How easy to be a superhero when you had special powers! And how impossible when you were only human.

Presently he heard a crash. He jumped up in time to see a leg dressed in silver shoes and striped stockings tumble down the chimney and hop beside the chair, where it stood at attention.

Bing-bang-bong! A second leg dropped down and, flexing itself, bounded over to the first.

Hsshhhh! The copper chest sprang open, and out popped a left arm and a right arm, both sleeved in green velvet. They fluttered to the chair with a swimming motion and drifted a short distance above the legs.

Thump. Out of the chest toppled the torso, in a doublet of green feathers. It settled itself on the legs and allowed the arms to join it, one at each side.

"I hope you play checkers," said Arcimboldo's voice, close by.

"Yes," quavered Anatole, "but couldn't you please put on your head?"

"You know, I was sure you'd run away," continued the voice. "And if you run, you forfeit the game."

From the ceiling floated the head of a green bird with a long, sharp beak.

"When I'm at home, I wear my real head," explained Arcimboldo.

He took a pair of gold-rimmed glasses from his doublet and set them carefully on his beak. From the glasses dangled a silver string. He unfastened the string very carefully and tossed it to the owl, who caught it in her beak and flew from Anatole's shoulder to Arcimboldo's.

"If you want the thread of death, you must win it fair and square," said the magician.

"Did you win it fair and square?" asked Anatole.

"I bought the secret of winning it from a cockroach," answered Arcimboldo. "I gave him all the gold he could carry."

And he tapped the golden cockroach that swung on a thin chain around his neck. A cockroach in a turban and a ragged coat; Anatole recognized her at once as the mistress of the Trading Post.

"Never trust a traitor," said Arcimboldo, "not even a helpful traitor. The first move is yours, Anatole."

Anatole put out his hand to make the first move and hesitated.

*"From the ceiling floated the head of a green bird
with a long, sharp beak."*

"Just a minute, Arcimboldo. If you get to wear your magic glasses, I get to wear *my* magic glasses. That's fair and square."

"*Your* magic glasses?" exclaimed Arcimboldo, frowning.

"I wouldn't be caught dead without my magic glasses," said Anatole. And he took his glasses out of his pocket and put them on.

Then, with a great show of confidence, he moved his first piece one square.

"Arcimboldo, I'm sorry for you. I'm not called 'Four Eyes the Fierce' for nothing."

Arcimboldo studied the board and stole glances at his opponent's face. The boy was smiling.

"Anatole, I'm sorry for you, too. So sorry, in fact, that I'm willing to play without my magic glasses if you'll play without yours."

"Not a chance," said Anatole.

"Fair and square, Anatole. We play without glasses or we don't play."

"Oh, Arcimboldo," said Anatole, "you don't know what you're asking."

"No glasses, or no game."

"We must take them off together, then. One, two, three."

At the count of three, both took off their glasses and tucked them out of sight. Anatole squinted at the board, though in truth he saw it very well, for he was nearsighted and could always see what was close to him. The army of pearl checkers shone on the emerald squares. Arcimboldo's emerald pieces glowed sullenly, green on green.

"Emeralds for me. Pearls for you," said Arcimboldo.

The silence in the room deepened. It seemed to Anatole that everything in the room, from the largest church bell to the smallest sleigh bell, was holding its breath.

Arcimboldo moved an emerald. "Your turn," he said.

Anatole was about to make his move when a crackling and a sizzling all around him made him draw back in alarm. Before his eyes, Arcimboldo turned into one giant flame, which danced on the emerald bench and gave off the most terrible heat. A faint moaning and humming swept through the bells. The owl beat her wings, and the searing wind they stirred took Anatole's breath away.

"Do you feel the need of a fan now, Anatole, when all creation can scarcely draw a breath?" whispered the magician. "Oh, if you had that fan now, you would thank Arcimboldo from the bottom of your heart."

Anatole was too parched to speak. It took all his strength to move a single pearl. The instant he did so, a roar as of rushing water filled the room. The fire sizzled out without leaving so much as a single ash, and now there whirled about on Arcimboldo's bench a giant waterspout, which sent wave after wave into the room. The bells rocked and clanged in muffled voices, and the table, the chest, the benches, and the checkerboard were tossed up and down. The waves broke over

Anatole's head, pulled him into their churning depths, and threw him out again, but he clung to his seat and shouted, "Your turn, Arcimboldo—your turn!"

The waves retreated, the waterspout vanished, and Anatole saw, as Arcimboldo took on his own shape and made his move, that not a single piece on the board had been disturbed. Anatole took one of the magician's emeralds, the magician took one of Anatole's pearls. In a silence so total that every sound in the universe seemed to have withdrawn from this place, Anatole and Arcimboldo played the game out till only a few pieces remained on the board.

"Your turn, Anatole."

When Anatole lifted his hand to move, a blast of cold air froze him to his seat. He tried to think of his next move, but his head felt crammed with pictures, as if somebody inside were turning the pages of a vast book. Here was Uncle Terrible's apartment and the little house, and here was the Trading Post under the floorboards and the rutabaga lamp in Mother's house, and here was his own mother kissing him good-by and his father kissing him also and saying, "Take my knapsack, Anatole, take my knapsack!"

"Your move, Anatole," said Arcimboldo. "What a splendid bell you'll make! I shall hang you in a place of honor."

Ice glittered on the walls and on the wings of the owl and on the bells—and what was Arcimboldo himself now but an iceberg, turning slowly on the bench, sending out its cold breath to freeze him?

Place of honor, place of honor. The words repeated themselves in Anatole's head. He looked down hopefully at the board. His own breath sent little clouds of steam over it.

Thump, thump. Was Rosemarie here, skipping invisibly among the bells?

No. It was the racing of his own heart.

Thump.

The emeralds on the board flashed at him. He thought of Uncle Terrible, imprisoned in the body of the serpent, and how cold the world would be without him. And without Rosemarie. His mind cleared, and he made his last move. The pearl took the last emerald on the board. Over the pealing of bells he heard himself shouting, "I've won, Arcimboldo. I've won!"

"Fair and square," sneered Arcimboldo. And he gave a long mocking laugh. Anatole saw a door open and the owl, clasping the thread of death in her beak, flutter into the air and sailed outside.

Anatole jumped up and ran after her. When he crossed the threshold, he was blinded by the brilliance of trees. Steel they were—bark, branches, all steel—and on every tree hung ivory apples that gleamed through the copper leaves like young moons ripening under the red sky. The owl was skimming the tops of the trees.

All at once she wheeled back, as if something had caught her eye, and alighted in a steel thicket ahead of him. He heard a shriek, a hiss, a beating of wings, and much crashing about in the underbush.

The owl uttered a mournful whistle and flew off toward the magician's house, but Anatole could see that she no longer carried the thread in her beak. Then Anatole heard a voice call after her, "That will teach you to eat your betters, madam."

To Anatole's astonishment, the voice began humming "Blue Moon." Parting the branches, he spied a snake on whose skin shimmered all the colors of the rainbow, sunning himself by a small pool.

"Uncle Terrible!" shouted Anatole.

Startled into a panic, the snake fled straight into the pool.

"Come back," called Anatole, and he plunged his hands into the water after it. To his dismay, the silver serpent ring slid from his finger and sank as swiftly as if summoned by the water itself.

The next moment, out crawled Uncle Terrible.

"Oh, marvelous pool!" cried Uncle Terrible. "Whoopee!"

Nothing was left of the snake but its skin, draped over Uncle Terrible's arm.

"Uncle Terrible, I'm so glad you're here."

"And so am I, Anatole. You didn't see me, following you in the orchard?"

Anatole shook his head.

"The thread of death," said Uncle Terrible. "Do you have the thread of death?"

"The owl must have dropped it," said Anatole.

Uncle Terrible threw away the snakeskin, and they began to search on hands and knees. Presently a kindly voice inquired, "Is it silver?"

Anatole and Uncle Terrible looked at each other in alarm.

"Is it silver?" repeated the voice. "Of course, I've no use for silver. You've nothing to fear from me."

Suddenly they both saw the thread, half covered by the snakeskin, sparkling on a fern.

"Arcimboldo is playing a trick on us," whispered Anatole.

"He doesn't need to play any more tricks," said Uncle Terrible. "He knows we'll never find our way out."

The voice spoke again.

"I believe I could fly you out. You still don't see me? I'm right at your feet."

At their feet rested the fern.

"Do the plants in this forest talk?" exclaimed Anatole.

"I don't know," said the fern, very humbly. "These are the first words I've ever said to anyone."

"Perhaps the snakeskin—" began Uncle Terrible.

And Anatole, who was also thinking of the snakeskin, lifted it away and said to the fern, "Speak."

The fern was mute. Anatole laid the snakeskin on it once more.

"Can you speak now?"

"As I was saying," continued the fern, "I come from a large family. Do you see my relatives waving all around the pool? Gather some of us together and bind us into wings with your silver thread."

"What if the wings don't work?" mused Uncle Terrible.

"Oh, but Uncle Terrible," said Anatole, "what if they *do*?"

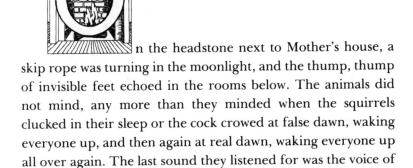n the headstone next to Mother's house, a skip rope was turning in the moonlight, and the thump, thump of invisible feet echoed in the rooms below. The animals did not mind, any more than they minded when the squirrels clucked in their sleep or the cock crowed at false dawn, waking everyone up, and then again at real dawn, waking everyone up all over again. The last sound they listened for was the voice of the invisible girl singing them into oblivion:

> "Bottom, bottom, dish clout,
> Dutch cheese and sauerkraut.
> Our first lieutenant was so neat
> He stopped in the battle to wash his feet."

The possums, who had never seen a lieutenant, spread the rumor that the first lieutenant—and the ancestor of all other lieutenants—had had a pink snout and a long thin tail like theirs. The tiger cat knew that only a cat would stop in the battle to wash his feet, but he kept this information to himself.

"Igamu, ogamy, box of gold,
  A louse on my head was seven years old.
  I inched him and pinched him and made his back smart,
  And if I ever catch him, I'll tear out his heart,"

sang Rosemarie, skipping.

She shared a room with a mole, an elk, and a raccoon. The mole and the raccoon and Rosemarie claimed the bed close to the fire. It was carved to resemble a brake of ferns. The elk, who was a light sleeper, dozed on a fragrant heap of straw, a safe distance from flying sparks.

The mole slept with his glasses perched on his nose and his paws folded together on his stomach. He was always the first to retire. Lying on his back with his eyes shut, he prayed, "Mother of Moles, Father of Ferrets, Sister of Shrews, Brother of Beavers, Spirit in all of us, whoever you are, bless Anatole. Also, I beg you to improve my eyesight. Amen."

After the mole had settled himself, Rosemarie hung her skip rope on the bedpost and curled up beside him and wished she could grow clothes as soft as his fur. Then it was the elk's turn. The other two could hear him pacing round and round, treading the straw flat.

When the raccoon came in, she blew out the lamp.

Last of all, the bed itself would breathe a lullaby that soothed them like the wind rustling in the leaves that the bed once had when long ago it grew as a tree on Himmel Hill.

> Moonlight, starlight,
> The bogeyman's not out tonight.
> Wash your bones
> With precious stones—

Soon only Rosemarie lay awake. She listened to the crackling of the fire and the pleasant bustle of animals in the surrounding rooms. Through the open door, she watched the shadows of the nighthawks as they spread their wings before the Great Fire in Mother's room, not understanding that the Great Fire warmed everyone in the house. Rosemarie thought of Anatole and the doves on the roof at home. She thought of Arcimboldo the Marvelous, and then she thought of her grandmother, who did not like to sleep and who made omelets at midnight and wrote long letters to friends, both dead and alive, and asked Rosemarie to mail them.

At last Rosemarie climbed out of bed, tiptoed past her sleeping friends, picked up her skip rope, and crept up the stairs into the chilly air of the upper world. The raccoon always sensed when she was gone and followed her. He sat on a marble lamb and said, "Don't pay any attention to me. I don't want to make a nuisance of myself."

"You're never a nuisance," said Rosemarie.

Thump, thump, thump. The rope slapped the headstone on which Rosemarie was skipping.

"I'd give anything to know as much as you do, Rosemarie," said the raccoon, sighing.

"You would? Do those rings on your tail come off?"

"In my great-great-grandfather's time, all raccoons could take off their rings. But there's not a raccoon alive today who remembers the way of doing it."

"Now I'm jumping backward with my arms crossed," said Rosemarie.

"You're wonderful. Simply wonderful," said the raccoon.

"Thank you," said Rosemarie.

"It breaks my heart that the otters don't believe in you," said the raccoon. "Except Elder Otter. He believes. The others say you're nothing but an enchanted rope."

"They've got some nerve," said Rosemarie.

"I told them about the wind. I said, 'You don't see the wind, but you see what it does. Our invisible girl is as real as the wind.' "

"I'm a lot realer than the wind," said Rosemarie. "Tell them I've got a mother and a father and a grandmother, and I live in an apartment with a garden, and I go to Sacred Heart Elementary School."

"They'll never believe me. Except Elder Otter."

"Tell them I'm in the advanced math class."

"I'll try," said the raccoon. "If only they'd talk to you at night the way I do."

Thump, thump.

"Will you still talk to me when you can see me?" asked Rosemarie.

"Always and always," replied the raccoon.

"What do you think I look like?"

"You have bright eyes, lovely pointed ears, short silver fur, and a tail more beautiful than I can imagine."

"A tail!" exclaimed Rosemarie.

"Are you laughing at me?" asked the raccoon in sorrowful tones.

"No," said Rosemarie. She was glad the raccoon couldn't see her smiling.

It was Elder Otter who complained to Mother about Rosemarie. He crept to Mother's bed right after the cock crowed at false dawn.

"We all have our little tasks, Mother," he whispered. "We otters fish for you, the rabbits gather greens for your table, the cock puts your lamp to sleep at sunrise, the spiders mend, the elks fetch and carry—oh, I could go on and on. And what does *she* do? She sits by the well and watches the water."

"That's her job," said Mother. "To watch the water."

"Why does she get to watch the water?"

"Because she knows what to watch for."

"You think I don't know what to watch for?"

"He crept to Mother's bed right after the cock crowed at false dawn."

"Look into the water, Elder Otter, and tell me what you see," said Mother.

Elder Otter scampered to the far corner of Mother's room and crouched at the rim of the well. In that plain room, which held nothing else but the Great Fire dancing in its ring of stones, the well sparkled like an enormous eye.

"What do you see?" asked Mother.

"I see a young trout, more silver than is common, and a pair of young carp, more gold than I'm used to."

"Fish," said Mother. "Is that all you see?"

"That's all there is to see, Mother," said Elder Otter.

"Rosemarie sees more," said Mother. "Rosemarie sees Anatole."

After breakfast, Rosemarie went as usual to Mother's room and sat by the well. She thought of Anatole and of the serpent who called himself Uncle Terrible, and up from the darkness at the bottom of the well swam a picture, which spread itself on the surface of the water like oil. The mole sat beside her to keep her company. Today the raccoon joined them, and it was he who first spied two shadows tossing among the stars.

"Mother, Mother!" called the raccoon. "I see Anatole flying! And I see a stranger flying beside him."

"That's Uncle Terrible," said Mother, bending over the water. "He's got his own shape back. He found himself in one of my wells."

"You have wells in the magician's house, Mother?" asked the raccoon, much surprised.

"I have wells everywhere for those who can find them."

Now all four watchers leaned over the image. It quivered a little. In the water-picture, snow was beginning to fall, clearing the street of colors.

"I know that street," said Rosemarie, "but I don't know the name of it."

She was certain she'd passed that blackboard hanging in the shop window, on which was written:

TODAY'S SPECIAL: FLOUNDER!

And the Ebony Beauty Parlor next door, with the face of a black girl framed in a halo of hair. And the tailor shop next door to that:

CICERO YIN, ALTERATIONS

In his window stood a photograph of John F. Kennedy, and behind the photograph a large jade tree spread its plump leaves in all directions.

Under Rosemarie's eager gaze, the two travelers alighted on the roof, several flights above the tailor's shop. She saw Anatole and Uncle Terrible open the skylight and climb in. An owl glided down, peered into the skylight, gave a cluck of satisfaction, and, with a fierce beating of wings, clattered into the air and flew off toward the magician's house.

"She's clumsy," said the raccoon. "She hasn't been an owl long."

"Did she ride in the taxi with me?" asked Rosemarie.

"Yes," said Mother. "And she's going to tell Arcimboldo what she's just seen—what we've just seen."

"She's working for *him*, then?" asked the raccoon.

The water grew dark once more.

"Can't we help them, Mother?" asked the mole.

"Yes. But we must watch for our chance. Watch. Watch."

natole sat up and rubbed his knee. The room into which they had fallen was very cold and so tiny that when Uncle Terrible stood up, his head brushed the ceiling.

"Are you injured?" asked Uncle Terrible.

"No," said Anatole, and in the same instant both of them saw what had hurt him: a large iron ring anchored to a door in the floor.

Uncle Terrible gave a whoop of joy. Together they grabbed the ring and pulled.

Below them lay another room, much larger, also empty, and another trap door exactly like the first. First Anatole and then Uncle Terrible jumped down and tried to pull open this door also. It did not budge.

"Pull harder," said Uncle Terrible, and the door broke free.

Anatole knelt, and Uncle Terrible squatted beside him,

holding it lest it should slam shut and wake the tailor below. A rush of warm air rose to meet them.

They were looking directly into the shop itself. Here was the jade plant and the back of the framed picture of John F. Kennedy, and behind the cash register a partition which hid the workshop from the view of customers. But nothing was hidden from Anatole and Uncle Terrible, who saw below them the tailor's worktable and the pegboard on which he hung his threads, as bright and various as the feathers of birds, and his portable sewing machine and his straight-backed chair. His shears and electric iron gleamed on the worktable. The shelf behind the table was crammed with bolts of cloth and books, which bulged with swatches and patterns. Tacked over the empty clothes rack was a sign:

FINISHED WORK

"Let's go down," said Anatole.

"My dear Anatole," exclaimed Uncle Terrible. "Do you think I'm Superman? Able to leap tall buildings at a single bound?"

"Then I'll go alone," said Anatole. And holding fast to the snakeskin, he climbed through the trap door and let himself down.

He landed—thud!

The spools, the shears, the threads—everything trembled. Out of sight in a room beyond this one, Anatole heard pots and dishes rattle.

"Can you find where he keeps his golden needles?" Uncle Terrible called softly.

Anatole lifted the books and patterns and swatches one after another. Nothing under them but a Chinese newspaper. He peered behind bolts of tweed and twill and gabardine.

Nothing. Nothing.

He tiptoed to the room at the back and found himself in the tailor's kitchen, which smelled pleasantly of ginger. Past the stove, the icebox, the table big enough for one, to yet another door—ah, here was the tailor himself, fast asleep in his bed, his teeth shining in a glass of water on the nightstand.

The tailor sighed and turned over on his stomach. His breathing moved the covers up and down, up and down.

Anatole hurried back to Uncle Terrible.

"I can't find the needles."

"If only the shears could speak," said Uncle Terrible, "or the sewing machine. They'd tell us."

"But they can speak," said Anatole, and he laid the snakeskin on the sewing machine.

The sewing machine gave a hoarse wheeze of astonishment.

"Can you please tell me," said Anatole, "where the tailor keeps his golden knitting needles?"

"Mrrrrssssrs," answered the machine. "Krrrwwwwooow."

Hastily Anatole took away the snakeskin for fear the machine would wake the tailor and laid it on the pegboard over the threads. The threads all began to chatter at once in shrill voices.

"Can you tell me where the tailor—" began Anatole, but they did not hear him; they had too many quarrels to settle with one another. Again he took the snakeskin away.

"I'll try the shears," he said, feeling rather desperate, for the window showed him the blue light of early morning.

And he laid the snakeskin on the shears.

The shears clip-clapped, once, twice.

"At last," murmured the shears in an oily voice. "At last I'm appreciated. After thirty years of service, I can tell my story."

"Please, can you tell me—"

"I've walked for miles and miles," continued the shears, "up velvet and down linen, over the gabardine highway, along the satin turnpike, and where has it gotten me?" And the shears clapped its two halves together like legs.

"Please," said Anatole. "I need the tailor's golden needles. It's a matter of life and death."

"Can't help you, can't help you," said the shears. "The tailor sleeps with them every night in his pocket, and now he's got them working on a magnificent cape, and he keeps both the needles and cape in bed with him. Keeps an eye on things, keeps an eye on things."

Anatole cast a longing glance at the tailor's bedroom, and the shears clip-clapped once, twice, and said, "If you're thinking of stealing them, think again. They won't go. They'll screech at you, jab you, stab you—oh, think again. They're spoiled things. Brought up among royalty. Think themselves finer than the rest of us."

Anatole considered this remark.

"Does the tailor need an apprentice?" he asked.

"There's only one thing the tailor needs," replied the shears.

"What?" called down Uncle Terrible.

The shears gave a little shriek of alarm.

"Who's that hiding in the ceiling?"

"That's my friend," said Anatole. "You can tell him."

For several minutes the shears would not speak but only clipped the air nervously. At last the oily voice resumed. "A cat. That's what he needs. The mice in this building are driving him crazy."

Anatole felt his right wrist tingle.

"A cat!" repeated Uncle Terrible. "We have no cat. We are undone."

"No, we're not, Uncle Terrible," said Anatole. He held up his right hand and shook it. Something unwound itself and hung there, grinning.

It was the face of a cat, black from the ears to the nose, with a white chin and two dark spaces for the eyes.

"Mother said if I put it on, I'll be a cat for twenty-four hours," said Anatole.

"Anatole, don't," said Uncle Terrible. "Don't put on that mask."

"Take care of this," said Anatole, and he tossed the snakeskin into the air. It floated up, up, and curled itself into Uncle Terrible's hand. The thread of death he untied from his waist and wound around his finger.

"Anatole—" said Uncle Terrible.

But Anatole was already slipping the mask over his face.

The instant he did so, his ears shrank to pointed tents, whiskers crisp as celery sprang from his cheeks, and his whole body sank low as a footstool and grew fur, nicely patterned in black and white like a tuxedo. His tail stood up straight as a wand.

He flicked the tail to get the feel of it. He bowed and stretched his paws and discovered his claws. They gleamed, then disappeared into the wonderful sheaths at the tip of each paw. Wrapped around a claw on his right paw, the thread of death might have been a dustball, a feather, a scrap of tweed.

Anatole scampered into the tailor's bedroom and bounded to the foot of the bed. He heard the trap door close. He tucked his paws under him and waited for the tailor to wake up.

The street noises began: cars passed the tailor's shop, a bus groaned and stopped, groaned and started. Women's voices drew near and faded away. The tailor sat up. He saw the cat at the foot of the bed, and his mouth fell open.

"Good morning," said Anatole.

"A talking cat! Mother of God!" cried the tailor.

He sprang out of bed and darted into the far corner of the bedroom. And wonder of wonders, right behind him danced twelve golden needles, and on the needles danced the golden cloak of Arcimboldo the Marvelous, and the needles were clacking away, for they never wasted a moment from the time the tailor opened his eyes to the time he closed them.

"Didn't you wish for a talking cat?" asked Anatole.

The tailor squeezed himself behind the nightstand, and what a strange figure he made, hugging himself in his nightshirt while the cloak gathered itself around him and the needles went on knitting, click, click, click.

"Think hard," said Anatole. "Didn't you wish for a talking cat? Because if there's been a mistake, I can go back where I came from."

Though the tailor was terribly frightened, he did not want to lose so rare a companion as a talking cat. He put his teeth in and adjusted them.

"I have often wished for a cat since my old cat died," said the tailor. "But I don't think I ever wished for a talking cat."

"I'm the deluxe model," said Anatole. "And I'll stay with you and catch your mice and keep you company, on one condition."

"What condition?" asked the tailor.

"Never tell anyone I can talk."

"I won't tell a soul," said the tailor.

"And now," said Anatole, "if you'll be so kind as to bring me my breakfast."

"Of course," said the tailor.

And he bustled joyfully about the tiny kitchen, lit the gas burner, and set the table with two white porcelain bowls, one for himself and one for Anatole.

"Grape Nuts?" he asked. "My old cat loved Grape Nuts."

"I love Grape Nuts," said Anatole.

They ate in silence, the tailor leaning forward on his stool, drinking tea with one hand and stroking Anatole with the other. From deep inside Anatole rose a purr, which surprised him, for he did not know he was making it. He had a most unfamiliar urge to wash his face. The tailor poured himself tea from the porcelain pot and said, "I shall call you Pai Shan. All my cats are called Pai Shan. You are the fourth to carry that name."

"And I shall call you Noble Master," said Anatole, because it seemed the proper thing to do.

The tailor looked perfectly delighted.

"Noble Master," said Anatole, "I've never before seen needles that knit by themselves. I suppose you take great care of them."

"Great care," said the tailor. "A thief tried to steal them once, and they nearly killed him. No matter where I go, they stick by me. Watch."

He rose from the table and walked out of the kitchen into the

"They ate in silence, the tailor leaning forward on his stool, drinking tea with one hand and stroking Anatole with the other."

workroom. The needles bobbed right after him, whisking the cloak behind them, and the clatter and clack of needle upon needle sounded like the grinding of teeth.

"They won't follow anyone else," the tailor said proudly.

"They are wonderful," said Anatole. "I suppose you got them from a great magician?"

"I got them from my father, who got them from his father, who was given them by the emperor of China, in exchange for making the empress's wedding gown."

"And where did the emperor get them?" inquired Anatole.

"Oh, that's a story," said the tailor, smiling. "When the emperor was an infant, his grandmother gave him a golden teething ring. When he grew up, he had all the teeth he wanted and no hope of cutting any more, so he had the ring melted down and forged into these needles."

The needles gathered themselves into a crown over the tailor's head, and the golden cloak slipped off and rolled down his shoulder in buttery waves.

"Is the cloak finished?" asked Anatole.

"All finished, and just in time," said the tailor. "Come, Delicious. Come, Winesap. Come, McIntosh, and Jonathan, and Rome Beauty. Come, Bonum and Fallawater and Yellow Newton and Fall Pippin and Russet and Northern Spy. Come, my most beautiful Gloria Mundi."

The tailor stroked Anatole between the ears.

"My father was fond of apples, but in China he seldom got

any. In America he liked to buy apples at the fruit stand on Orchard Street. The apple man always said, 'What kind do you want?' And when my father learned how many different kinds of apples grow in America, he could only say, 'How wonderful apples are!' and he named his needles after the apples. 'The needles are wonderful,' he would say, 'and the apples are wonderful too.' "

Bang, bang, bang!

"It's the wizard come for his cloak," exclaimed the tailor, and he tossed the cloak on the counter and, followed by the twelve golden needles, ran into the bedroom to fetch his clothes. Anatole seized the end of the cloak in his claws. So strong is the thread of life that the cloak did not tear, but row by row, from the bottom up, it began to unravel, and it was half gone by the time the tailor returned, pulling his trousers over his nightshirt.

But the tailor was too excited to notice. He opened the door, and the first customer of the day strode into the room, shaking the snow off himself like a dog.

 e looked exactly as Anatole had seen him in the coffee shop on the first day of his visit: red hair, red beard, and hunched into the same fur coat. He drew the collar around his face and the owl shifted her weight on his arm as he leaned forward and inspected the golden cape with keen eyes.

"Did you use all the thread?" asked Arcimboldo.

"All the thread, dear Arcimboldo," replied the tailor.

"You didn't break it? You didn't cut it?"

"My needles always do as they're told," said the tailor. "Try it on."

Arcimboldo shook out the cloak. It was collared in glory but hemmed in a snarl of golden thread. The tailor began to tremble.

"Dear Arcimboldo, five minutes ago the cloak was done. I myself laid it on the table."

"Dear Cicero Yin," sneered Arcimboldo, "have you any idea who unraveled it?"

The tailor hung his head.

"Dear, dear Cicero Yin, believe me, things are bad for you. You have a pair of demons in your attic."

"Demons!" cried the tailor.

"My owl saw two demons fly into your attic last night. Watch out, Cicero Yin. Lock your trap door tonight. Because if my cloak isn't finished by tomorrow morning, I'll turn you into a carrot and eat you alive."

Terrified, the tailor bowed deeply.

"I'm most grateful to your owl for warning me of my great danger. Honorable owl, may I reward you for your services?"

"I'd like a plate of shrimp on rice cakes," said the owl. "Right now."

And she flew from Arcimboldo's arm to the tailor's shoulder, and all the time he was picking the shrimp out of the jar, she nagged him, "More! More!" and "Duck sauce, I want duck sauce!" and "Noodles, more noodles," till he had given away both his lunch and his supper. Nor did she so much as thank him for setting his own bowl, heaped with delicacies, before her on the counter.

The owl fluttered to the bowl and gobbled up the shrimp. Anatole, watching her, thought of Uncle Terrible upstairs, who was surely starved by this time. He thought of the treachery of the owl, first at Arcimboldo's house and now at the tailor's, and the next moment he leaped on her and sank his teeth into her wing.

"Grab the cat—he'll kill her!" shrieked Arcimboldo.

The tailor seized Anatole and shook him, and Anatole opened his jaws and let the owl drop. He had no intention of killing her, but he hoped to keep her from flying, and the sight of her torn wing brought a purr to his throat.

"There's your culprit," howled Arcimboldo. "There's your villain. There's the demon who unraveled my cloak."

And he stared long and hard at Anatole. With his skill in magic, he saw right off that this cat was enchanted. The eyes of enchanted animals are full of that odd mixture of pain and humor found only in the eyes of human beings, and they always shine with longing to return to themselves.

"Put that cat out tonight, Cicero Yin, if you want to live the rest of your life as man. Your word—give me your word on it."

"People say that a great blizzard is—"

"A cloak or a carrot," said Arcimboldo. "Choose."

"Dear Arcimboldo, I—"

The wizard was tucking the owl into his fur coat, which made him appear to have two heads, one large and one small.

"I give you my word," faltered the tailor.

The thinnest twist of a smile lit Arcimboldo's face as he opened the door and stalked out, leaving the tailor clutching the fragment of cloak while his golden needles danced overhead.

Through the open door came the voices of children passing:

> "Hey, hey,
> Can't catch me.
> I'm sitting on top of
> The Christmas tree."

The golden needles paused in midair. Then they rushed toward the open door. The tailor ran after them, and a snowball hit him in the chest.

"Move on, move on!" shouted the tailor, and he slammed the door.

But the children only sang louder.

> "Liar, liar,
> Your pants are on fire.
> Your nose is as long
> As a telephone wire."

Now the needles threw themselves at the door, pitifully, like children begging to go outside and join the others.

"They'll follow anyone who sings nonsense," groaned the tailor, wiping his forehead with the sleeve of his nightshirt. "They've never forgotten their days as a teething ring. Nonsense always reminds them of their youth, when they never knew a day of work."

Anatole was too astonished to speak. But the tailor, calmer

now, took a tape measure from around his neck and measured the remnant of the golden cloak.

"If they work from now till tomorrow morning, they can finish the cloak. Now tell me, Pai Shan, did you unravel the golden thread?"

A helpful lie stood on the tip of his tongue, but Anatole remembered the spider's warning: *No one who lies or steals can command them.*

"I did."

"But would you do it again?"

"I might."

"Oh, Lord," said the tailor, sighing. "You'd better take the day off and sleep by the stove. You'll be cold enough tonight."

Anatole laid his head on his paws and dozed by the oven, but he did not sleep. He checked for the thread of death tied around his claws—it was quite safe. He listened to the tailor putting on his clothes and to the wind rising outside. When the wind dropped and the tailor shifted the position of the cloth, he heard, in the silence, the click-click of the golden needles, knitting the thread of life.

Presently he heard something else: a scratching behind the stove. He lifted his head and pricked up his ears. A brown mouse peeped out from behind the stove, caught Anatole's eye, and unfurled a white flag.

"Truce," it squeaked.

"Truce," said Anatole, who thought the mouse very cunning and would not have hurt it for the world.

Five more mice stepped out and bowed deeply.

"We hope," said the mouse holding the flag, "that for a suitable reward we may maintain our old pact."

"What pact?" asked Anatole.

"Our pact with the cats in this house. The last three cats always left us a tenth part of their supper behind the stove. We in turn promised to disturb nothing in the tailor's cupboards. Naturally, there is compensation." The mouse cleared its throat. "A selection of monthly premiums."

"Premiums?"

"The treasures of the hunt. Leif Langhal, show him the premiums."

A young mouse with a very long tail came forward, lugging a silver brooch wrought in the shape of three baby birds in a nest. Both birds and nest were pocked with holes.

"Real diamonds," said Leif Langhal.

"But they've all fallen out," said Anatole.

"You don't *like* the brooch?" exclaimed Leif Langhal, surprised. "We were sure you'd like the brooch. Cats generally like birds."

"Haven't you anything else?" asked Anatole.

The mice whispered among themselves for a few minutes, and Leif Langhal was heard to protest, "That's an awful lot of

"*A young mouse with a very long tail came forward,
lugging a silver brooch . . .*"

work," and the others whispered, "Sssssshhhhh," and Leif Langhal said, "Well, hang it all, if I had a wagon to carry it in and a crane to lift it—" and the others pinched him till he squeaked, and the sewing machine stopped sewing. The tailor cocked his head—had he heard mice?

No. He heard nothing but the clack-clack of his faithful needles.

"Don't you have anything besides a brooch with the stones picked out?" asked Anatole.

"Only a book," said the mouse with the flag. "An old book that Leif picked up at the cockroachs' bazaar. We rarely trade with them. So much of their merchandise is enchanted. But the book can't harm any of us, for of course we can't read. It's very handsome. An addition to any shelf. Here comes Leif—see for yourself."

Anatole could scarcely believe his eyes. In his paws, Leif was dragging Uncle Terrible's magic book.

"I agree to the pact," said Anatole. "On one condition."

The mice exchanged uneasy glances.

"The trap door in the ceiling of the workroom will be locked tonight. Do you know another way up to the room?"

"Yes, indeed," said a plump gray mouse. "There are three passages leading directly to the loft."

"But they're blocked with plaster," said Leif Langhal, "and we'll have to clear one. That's an awful lot of work."

"How long will it take to clear one?" asked Anatole.

"We could finish it by midnight, I think," said the gray mouse.

"Listen, brothers," said Anatole. "A friend of mine is hiding in that loft. I want you to take him this book and bring him here. Tell him that the golden needles will follow anyone who sings nonsense. And show him how to find the Grape Nuts and the tea. He never skips breakfast, and he hasn't eaten for ages."

"Is your friend a mouse?" asked Leif Langhal.

"No, he's even bigger than the tailor. But very soon he will be no taller than yourselves."

The tailor pushed back his chair, and the mice slipped behind the stove.

"Remember," murmured a voice, light as a baby's breathing, "the tenth part of your supper. To be left behind the stove."

"I'll remember," said Anatole.

That evening the tailor ate no supper. He sat at his kitchen table, the tears running down his face, with Anatole on his lap, and he fed Anatole bites of cold chicken from his own hand, saying, "Take a little more, dear Pai Shan. Take a little more."

Beside them, the tailor's old radio sputtered the seven-o'clock news. The news was all weather: "Snow will continue into the evening—*crackle, crackle*. It's ten below in the city, temperature falling fast—*crackle*—windy and colder tonight. Arctic winds of fifty miles an hour are blowing this way from the northwest. Twenty-three inches of snow predicted—"

The tailor snapped it off.

"You're putting me outside in winds of fifty miles an hour?" cried Anatole.

The tailor whisked out his handkerchief and blew his nose. "I'll give you my scarf and a box to creep into— I'll give you a box—"

And he hurried into the workroom to find a box. Soon Anatole heard a great pounding. The tailor was nailing the trap door shut. Anatole put his nose to the place where the stove met the wall and called softly, "Leif!"

Silence. At last a small voice answered him.

"What do you want?"

"I have an important errand for you. Come out."

Leif Langhal appeared, looking rather sleepy and a little frightened. "What's the errand?"

"Do you know where Himmel Hill is?"

"All animals know where Himmel Hill is."

"And Mother's house? Do you know how to find it?"

"Don't *you* know how to find it? We're born knowing that."

"I need somebody to carry a message to Mother—somebody with wings. I need somebody who can fly to Mother's house and tell everybody in it to come here right away."

Leif stared at him, stupefied.

"Find me somebody to carry this message," pleaded Anatole, "and I shall ask my friend in the loft to give you a . . . a pound of Cheddar cheese."

"A pound!" squeaked Leif Langhal. "Why, so much cheese

would not fit through our door. We would have to chop it into a great many pieces, and that would be an awful lot of work."

"Half a pound then," said Anatole. "And I'll chop it up for you."

Leif Langhal closed his eyes for so long that Anatole feared he was falling asleep.

"I know a dove," Leif Langhal said in a dreamy voice. "She lives in a dovecote on a roof not far from here. But she wouldn't go out tonight. Not in this weather."

Through Anatole's head flashed the dovecote in the garden at the top of the fire escape. How desolate the rooftop must look now, the flowers dead under the snow, the grape arbor a white tunnel.

"The starling," murmured a voice. "Ask the starling who lives in the ventilation shaft."

Behind Leif Langhal appeared the plump gray mouse.

"Wait in the alley by the back door tonight," said the gray mouse. "We'll call the starling."

A footfall sent the two mice scurrying for shelter. The tailor stooped and picked up Anatole, stroked him behind the ears, tied his own scarf around his neck, and carried him tenderly to the front door.

"I've made a box for you outside," said the tailor. "Forgive me, Pai Shan. Please forgive me."

The door closed behind him, and as if it had been lying in wait for him all this time, the wind charged at Anatole full force. The box that the tailor had set out, lined with his own pillow, hurtled itself down the street just as though it were running away, and the tailor's scarf unwound itself from Anatole's neck and writhed into the air and vanished in a swirl of snow. Already the cars and the fire hydrant had the heavy shapelessness of clay things made by a beginner. Ice crystallized at the edge of his fur. He had not known ice could be so heavy or so cold.

By the time he reached the back door, he could scarcely breathe. Then a chillier thought struck him: tomorrow, in the first light of morning, he would be a child once more. A child in sneakers and a denim jacket. If Mother did not come, he would certainly freeze to death with the thread of death in his hand. And if he called for help, who over the howling of the wind could hear him?

Huddled in the alley, he dreamed himself in front of the fireplace at home after his bath, and part of him thought how much he would love a hot bath—that was the child part of him—and part of him thought, Could anything be worse than a hot bath? That was the cat part of him, and so he dreamed this way and that, now wanting one thing, now the other, till a voice at his ear roused him: "He can't go."

Anatole opened his eyes. By the back door, through a chink between the bricks, peeped Leif Langhal.

"Who can't go?"

"The starling. We found him on the roof, frozen to death."

"There must be somebody who can go," cried Anatole.

"There is," said the mouse, "but she's not very reliable. She lives in the loft."

"A bird?" asked Anatole.

"A bat," said the mouse. "But she's awfully dopey. They're always like that when they're hibernating. And she's never seen snow before."

"Where is she?" asked Anatole.

The mouse pointed straight up. On the rail of the upstairs porch hung a fat black pear, blowing in the wind.

"Can she carry a message?" Anatole asked doubtfully.

"She's very educated," said the mouse, "but at this time of the year she's a little queer in the head."

"Better her than no one," said Anatole. "Dear bat, come down."

"Don't call her down," warned the mouse. "She can't take off from the ground."

Anatole trudged up the stairs to the porch, and each stair froze his paws with a slick of ice hidden under the hummock of snow. Putting his mouth close to the bat's ear, Anatole shouted, "Can you hear me?"

"Um," said the bat, screwing up her face.

"I want you to fly to Himmel Hill. I want you to find Mother and the invisible girl. Tell the girl to bring her skip rope, and tell Mother and all the animals to come at once. And hurry."

"Give me room," muttered the bat in a thick voice.

She dropped from the railing, as if she had lost her grasp, but just before she hit the snow she swooped up and circled the roof twice.

"Go east!" called Anatole.

"I can only fly in circles," the bat called back. "But if I make my circles big enough"—the wind howled, and her voice grew very faint—"I shall certainly find—"

A gust of snow carried her off, and she was lost to sight.

The bat could see nothing but snow. This did not alarm her, however, for she was listening to the humming in the great still place all animals carry deep inside them that shows them their way over the most baffling distances. Birds and butterflies flying south, whales moving to warmer waters, stray dogs hunting for home—it is Mother's humming they listen for. If they make a wrong turn, they can scarcely hear it at all, and then they know they must turn another way. The bat heard it loud and clear, and she knew she could find Mother's house well enough.

But what of the wind that iced her wings? Mother could do nothing about that. From her childhood in a belfry, listening to sermons, the bat knew a great many proverbs, and in trying situations she recited them to herself, to keep up her spirits.

"A rolling bone gathers no sauce," murmured the bat. It did not sound quite right. "A bowling scone bathers no dross. No— A rolling stone gathers no moss. Now *that's* right," she told herself triumphantly, and pleased with her success, she tried another. "It's a shrill finned that throws no good. No— It's an ill wind that blows no good. Ah, in warm weather, on a summer's night I can say hundreds of them without missing a syllable. But in winter, when half of me is asleep, what can I expect?"

From far off she spied the rutabaga lamp. It shone amber in the window of Mother's room, as it always shines for those who look for it. She dipped low and glided toward it. The window opened, and she blew in and sank by the fire, exhausted.

Near her, by a well, sat a mole. And near the mole a rope was spinning round and round, and the thump, thump that the rope made when it struck the floor might have been the heartbeat of the invisible jumper that turned it.

"I have something to deliver," said the bat, panting a little.

Rosemarie stopped skipping, the rope fell to the floor, the mole sat up attentively.

"Oranges," said the bat. "It might have been oranges."

"Oranges?" repeated Rosemarie, and she picked up the bat, brought it close to the fire, and stroked it. The bat showed no surprise at being held by someone she could not see; there was so much in the world that she could not see with her weak eyes.

"Or lemons," murmured the bat.

"You don't remember what you came to deliver?" asked the mole.

"Eggs?" suggested Rosemarie. She tried to think of things that people might want delivered. "Newspapers? Milk?"

"Moss?" asked the mole.

"Or mail? Or messages?" asked Rosemarie.

"A message!" exclaimed the bat. "It's a message. And a very important message," she added. "Sell the churl to spring her flip soap and sell all the maminuls to chum at punce. And furry."

An astonished silence greeted this speech.

"That's the message?" said the mole.

"That's the gist of it," said the bat. "I may have got a few things scrambled."

"Could you say the message again?" asked Rosemarie. "We'll try to listen more carefully."

The bat closed her eyes. "Fell the burl to fling her pip pope and swell all the fainifuls to pum at dunce. And purry."

"Who sent you?" said Rosemarie.

"A mouse," replied the bat, "and a cat."

"Where did you meet this mouse and this cat?" asked Rosemarie.

"At the house of the skin-changer."

By this name are all tailors known to all bats, but the mole knew it too, for he had close friends among the bats.

"The tailor," said the mole. "She means the tailor."

"I've got it, I've got it," exclaimed the bat. "Tell the girl to bring her skip rope and tell all the animals to come at once. And hurry."

"Call Mother," said the mole. "Call the creatures."

That night the snow sprinkled the city with silence. It buried the bus stops, it built hummocks over the parked cars, it heaped hills over the entrances to the subways. Coffee houses, drugstores, butcher shops, bars closed down, and all the bustle and traffic of the city ceased.

Through the snowswept city moved the animals, padding, galloping, loping, flying, darting. Snow brushed their footprints and hushed their hoofbeats, and Mother marched behind them, the flames on her antlers beaming a path.

They passed the fish store. They passed the Ebony Beauty Parlor. At the dark door of Cicero Yin, the creatures stopped and huddled together. Half buried in the snow, which covered his stoop, a child's hand and a pair of feet poked out.

"Sneakers," clucked Mother, "in this weather."

"Oh, Mother, it's Anatole," cried Rosemarie, "and he's dead!"

The creatures crowded around him, and those in front licked the snow aside, and when his denim jacket appeared and then his face, so still and so pale, they bellowed and mewed and barked and howled, till Mother pushed her way past them. She didn't weep, not she. She folded her arms over her chest and

*"The creatures crowded around him, and those in front
licked the snow aside . . ."*

said severely, "Anatole, didn't I tell you to wear your boots? Didn't I tell you to button your jacket?"

And she picked him up in her arms and blew on his face, his hands, his feet. A faint flush came into them. He moved first one leg, then the other. When he opened his eyes, Mother set him on his feet. Everyone cheered.

"How cold I am," he whispered. "Mother, open the door."

Mother bowed her head, and the golden light her antlers threw on the door seemed to melt its heart. The lock sprang open with a sigh, the door opened, and the animals trooped in.

Uncle Terrible was dancing around the room in the golden cloak while the bare needles clapped over his head, and now he ran joyfully to meet them.

"The cloak of life is finished," he exclaimed. "But the cloak of death is not yet started. We'll rhyme those needles to work. They'll do anything for a bit of nonsense."

Anatole slid the thread of death from his finger and sang:

> "Mother, Mother, I am ill.
> Send for the doctor on the hill.
> Doctor, doctor, will I die?
> Yes, my dear, and so must I."

To the delight of everyone, the twelve golden needles danced forward, hooked themselves to the thread, and started to knit.

In his bedroom, the tailor slept and dreamed. He dreamed

that Arcimboldo the Marvelous was chasing him with a vegetable parer and shouting at him, louder and louder, till he shouted so loud that the tailor woke up.

"What do I hear?" he said to himself.

Not shouting. No. A thump, thump, thump like the tread of an enormous animal, accompanied by a chorus of queer voices, some cracked, some shrill, some deep, all joyful:

"How many years will I live?
One, two, three, four, five, six—"

Much alarmed, the tailor jumped out of bed, popped in his teeth, and pulled on his trousers. As he hurried to the door of his workroom, he met a troop of mice, and every mouse was skipping a rope cut from his own threads. When he arrived at the threshold, the tailor could scarcely believe his eyes. A giantess and a boy and a man and a great crowd of animals were skipping rope, and the ropes were all made of tweeds and twills and gabardines, and in the middle of the room, one rope—one *real* rope—was spinning faster than the rest around thin air. The golden needles were dancing themselves into a blur like spun honey. And while he watched, open-mouthed, a magnificent silver cloak floated from the needles to the floor in shimmering folds.

Before the tailor could ask any questions, a girl with long black braids and wearing a nightgown popped out of nowhere, right into the fastest rope, and the raccoon shouted, "Why, you're *human!*" and everybody else whooped and hollered.

"It's finished, the cloaks are finished!"

Mother gathered them up, the golden cloak on her right arm, the silver on her left.

"Make peace, you two," she said, and she tossed them into the air, and they stuck together as one fabric, and Mother threw it over her shoulders, just as a loud knocking shook the front door.

Everyone froze.

"It's Arcimboldo!" shrieked the tailor. "Give me that cloak, madam."

He tugged at it in vain. Mother towered over him like a tree.

"Don't be afraid, Cicero Yin. Anatole will settle with Arcimboldo, and I shall pull a little wool over his eyes. When he comes in, he'll see nobody but a young stranger behind the counter."

Bang, bang, bang.

"Open the door, Cicero Yin!"

Mother leaned over Anatole, laid the snakeskin on his shoulders, and put Uncle Terrible's magic book in his hand.

"Tell him the door is open. Don't forget to show him the book."

"The door is open, Arcimboldo," said Anatole, all a-tremble. "Come in."

Arcimboldo burst into the room, and Mother took from the pocket of her apron a handful of snow—and yet not snow, for real snow quickly melts in your pocket—and she flung it at the wizard and at the owl who rode on his shoulder. Anatole noted with satisfaction a Band-Aid on her wing.

"Where's the tailor?" roared Arcimboldo, and he pounded his fist on the counter.

"Yes, where's the tailor?" sneered the owl.

The tailor stood not four feet from both of them, quaking and shaking. The animals did not move; from hunting and being hunted, they knew how to remain perfectly still.

"I'm his helper," said Anatole. "Can I help you?"

"I've come for my cloak."

"For his cloak," croaked the bird.

"Can you wait just a minute?" asked Anatole.

"One minute." Arcimboldo drew out his pocket watch, and the death's-head engraved on the back winked at Anatole. "It is one minute of eight. At eight o'clock I keep my promise to the tailor, wherever he is. A carrot, a carrot."

Tick, tick, tick.

"The tailor says you're a wise man," said Anatole. "Now, I have a book here that I can't read."

"You can't read?" snapped the wizard. "Dumbbell."

"It's written in a foreign language," said Anatole. "The tailor says you know all languages. But I'll bet you don't know this one."

"Let's have a look," said the wizard.

He picked up the book and held it at arm's length, and Anatole quietly raised the flowers over the page while Arcimboldo read,

"Woneka, wonodo,
Eka mathaka rata—"

The owl spied a spill of Grape Nuts on the counter—Uncle Terrible had finished off the box—and she flew to the feast.

"A gbae se
Dombra, dombra, dombra."

Suddenly the lean figure of Arcimboldo disappeared. But on the counter, in front of Anatole, a very tiny Arcimboldo was shaking his fists and hopping up and down, knee-deep in the Grape Nuts.

Everyone was too astonished to move or speak, except the owl, who was so absorbed in her eating that she did not even look up. But she was heard to say, with immense satisfaction, "At last—a really fine mouse."

And before anyone could stop her, she plucked up Arcimboldo in her beak and ate him.

Then she too disappeared. And there in the shop stood the lady from Brooklyn in her curly fur coat, just as Anatole remembered her from the coffee shop. Finding herself transported to the tailor's shop in her bare feet, she looked about in bewilderment.

Outside, on every side, bells were ringing as if all the bells in the city were celebrating a great victory.

"The last spell is broken," said Mother. "The bells are saying good-by and fading into air. The prisoners of the bells are free. They are waking up in the places they left behind them. And the people who gave them up for lost are saying to one another, 'It's a miracle.'"

"Am I dreaming?" asked the woman from Brooklyn.

Mother laughed. "No. But as the sun climbs higher, you will forget this night, though many nights have passed in my country during this single night in yours. First you will forget Arcimboldo. Then you will forget Anatole and his friends. Last of all, you will forget me. You, dear lady, and you, Cicero, will say to yourselves, 'What a wonderful dream I had! If only I could remember it.' That is how it feels to come out of an enchantment."

"I hope I never forget you," said Anatole.

"Not everyone forgets me," said Mother.

The bells grew fainter and fainter and died away altogether. Mother tucked the magic book into her apron pocket and tied the snakeskin around her waist.

"You won't mind my taking these things, Uncle Terrible?"

"It's the least I can do for you," said Uncle Terrible, who was only too glad to be rid of them.

"Children," said Mother, "it is time to go home. My floor wants sweeping, and my lamp must be put to sleep at sunrise.

My creatures know the way to my house. But Anatole and Rosemarie and Uncle Terrible shall ride with me on my cloak."

"Are they going to Himmel Hill?" asked the raccoon, who did not want to leave Rosemarie.

"Not this time," said Mother. "Are you ready, Anatole? And Rosemarie? And Uncle Terrible?"

"Pardon me," squeaked a tiny voice, "but there was a promise of Cheddar."

A single leap carried Leif Langhal into the palm of Mother's hand.

"A cat whose face I do not see here promised us half a pound of Cheddar chopped into pieces for easy transport, in exchange for our services, faithfully rendered."

"Of course," said Mother.

She lifted her free hand, and a wheel of Cheddar dropped out and bounced toward the kitchen, pausing only long enough to break into twenty smaller wheels that rolled behind the stove and straight into the mousehole.

"All these marvels have exhausted me," said the bat. "If you'll excuse me, I'm going back to bed. Where *is* my bed?"

"Up there," said Mother, pointing to the trap door. Instantly the nails that closed it snapped in two. The door opened, and the bat flew straight up into the loft.

"Cicero Yin, the lady from Brooklyn wants the dress you promised her. What an eager customer, to come so early!"

As Mother spoke, she unfurled her cape, the golden side up.

It fluttered behind her on some secret breeze of its own.

"Get on board, children," sang Mother.

Anatole and Rosemarie climbed on. But Uncle Terrible hesitated, fearing that so frail a fabric could not possibly hold him.

"Don't worry, Uncle Terrible." Mother laughed. "There's room for many more."

It was an invitation he could not refuse. And when he had settled himself comfortably on the cape, with the two children on his lap, Mother opened the door of the shop.

She raised her hand and sent a single beam of light spinning through the dark like a ribbon of amber.

"There's your road, my darlings. Take care."

Anatole could not see the animals as they raced along the road. The light dissolved both their shapes and their shadows. But he could hear them barking and roaring and squeaking and thumping, and he heard the mole singing at the top of his voice,

> "The least of Mother's errands
> Is good enough for me,"

just as Mother rose into the air and soared, as slow and grand as a cloud, over the rooftops of the city.

Then her cloak billowed up and covered them.

". . . Mother rose into the air and soared,
as slow and grand as a cloud . . ."

ncle Terrible, we're home!"

She had set them down in Uncle Terrible's living room, beside the little house. The kitchen was swept and the table cleared. Anatole knew this was Mother's work, for she could not bear an untidy house.

Uncle Terrible rushed about, crowing for joy. "Here's my King Kong, and my Statue of Liberty, and, oh, here are my comics, safe and sound!"

He scooped up a *Superman* comic from the closet. On the cover, how tiny and bright and flat Superman looked as he leaped tall buildings with a single bound.

"I think we're the real superheroes," said Anatole.

"I think we are too," said Uncle Terrible.

From overhead they both heard it: thump, thump, thump.

"Can we invite Rosemarie to play with the little house?" asked Anatole.

*"She had set them down in Uncle Terrible's living room,
beside the little house."*

"Of course," said Uncle Terrible.

"I'll call her right away," said Anatole.

He climbed out on the fire escape. An orange light crept into the sky. Already the snow on the steps was melting. He ran up the steps two at a time.

When he reached the top, he looked down. Below him lay the church and the schoolyard, and higher and beyond, the television antennas that covered the rooftops like dead trees. Arcimboldo's trees, he thought. How long ago it all seemed to him now!

Far off gleamed the river. A train slipped past like a silver snake. The white turrets of Himmel Hill pricked the pale darkness, but a single light winked and flickered in the midst of them like a friendly star.

"Mother is putting her lamp to sleep," said Anatole, and he waved, just as the sun burst out of hiding and covered the lovely world at his feet with gold.